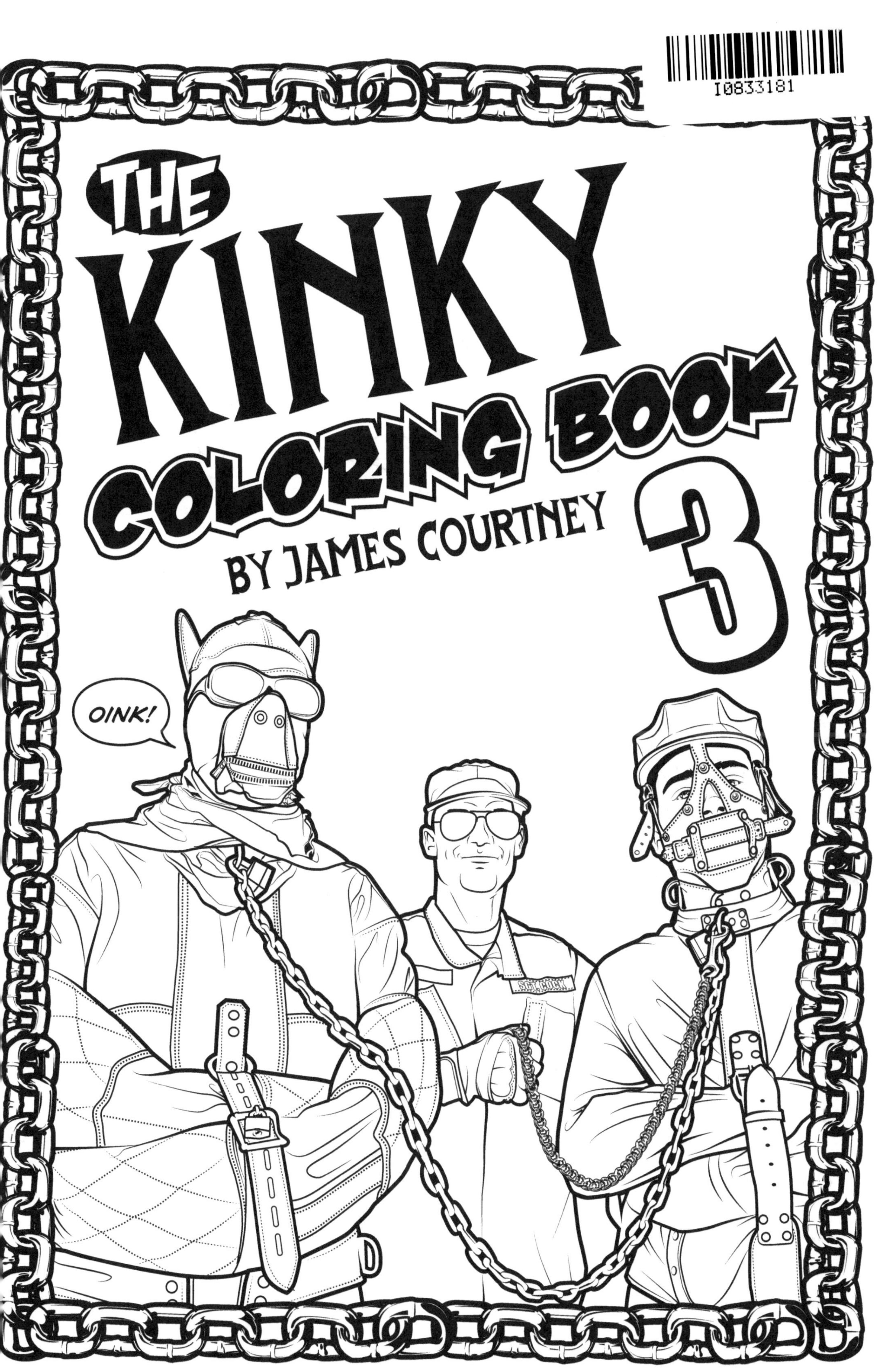
THE KINKY COLORING BOOK 3
BY JAMES COURTNEY
OINK!
SGT COCK

The Kinky Coloring Book 3
By James Courtney

ISBN 978-0-9858999-2-9

Dedicated to Meg and Lee, for all their friendship and support over the years.

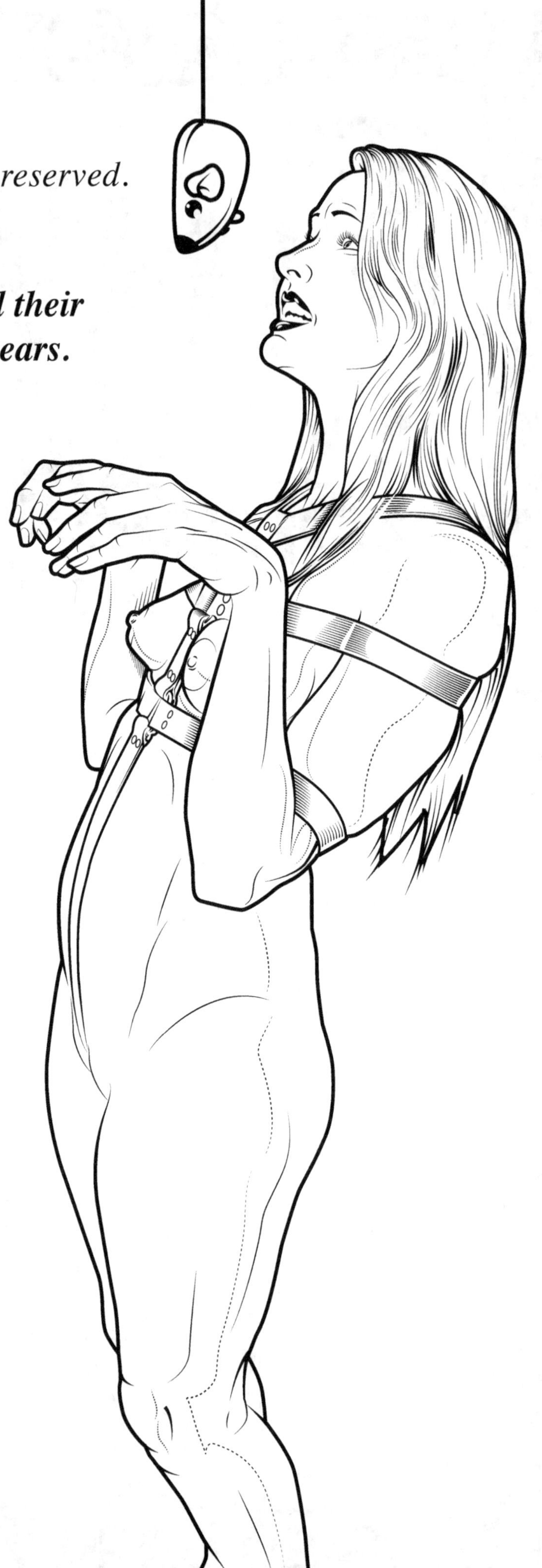

Nakedcomix.com
James Courtney
793 South Tracy Blvd #210
Tracy CA., 95376

Model: Raven Le Faye
Right Page,
Models: Christina and Maggie Mayhem
Front Cover,
Model: FreakyMar5

What gave you the idea to make a Kinky Coloring Book?

Some years ago, I wanted to do a coffee table book of my art. I was doing the research on self-publishing and, at the same time, I was running the numbers past the owner of my local comic book shop. He basically would shoot them down. He wasn't being mean; he pointed out that my price point would be higher than the books I would be competing against, so I would be losing money on the project.

One day I noticed that all his independent books were done in black and white. That, of course, is a much less expensive printing process. So, I asked, "What if I did a selection of black-and-white pieces and marketed it as a coloring book?" He liked that idea and told me that it would probably have a good chance of selling. So, that is how I got started.

How do you find your models?

In the beginning, I would ask models to work with me through web sites like Tribe, Model Mayhem or Fetlife. Now, many of my models are just people I've run across in the fetish scene, or they have come recommended by other photographers or models. It seems that nowadays it is less a case of me looking for them than it is them finding me. They either contact me through my Model Mayhem account or my website, Nakedcomix.

What do you look for in a model?

Attitude and enthusiasm score high in my book. Professionalism is very important, too. That's one reason why I don't do trades anymore. It is better to pay a model and know she/he will show up rather than renting studio time and having a no-show. I tend to like more experienced models for that reason also. I find that many newbies have a sense of daring that doesn't last past the first time you ask them to show their breasts. Still, I've worked with some first-time models who were confident in doing nudes and fetish, and excited by the concepts we are shooting. That makes things so much more fun during a long photo shoot. Working with a model is a collaboration. I mainly look for someone to partner with in order to make art.

What is your process for making the pictures?

I'll go through my collection of model photos and try to find a pose that strikes me as interesting. I'll then bring it into Adobe Illustrator and start drawing from it. Usually while working on the figure, I will get an idea for what to do with the background; that gets plugged in after I've finished the figure. In the beginning, I favored decorative graphic elements to make up my backgrounds. Lately, I find myself rising to the challenge of creating more illustrative and realistic environments for my figures. In the end, the purpose of the background is to compliment the figure in the drawing.

What do you want people to take away from your Kinky Coloring Books?

I want people to have fun with them! When we were young kids we used to do art, now we mostly just look at it. I want to give people art they can interact with and have a good time with. I've had people say they were scared to color the images because they were scared of ruining them. I tell them the images are incomplete until they are colored in. They are meant as a tool for fun rather than just something you keep pristine and untouched. I believe that no matter how beautiful the cake may be, in the end you have to eat it to really enjoy it.

James Courtney

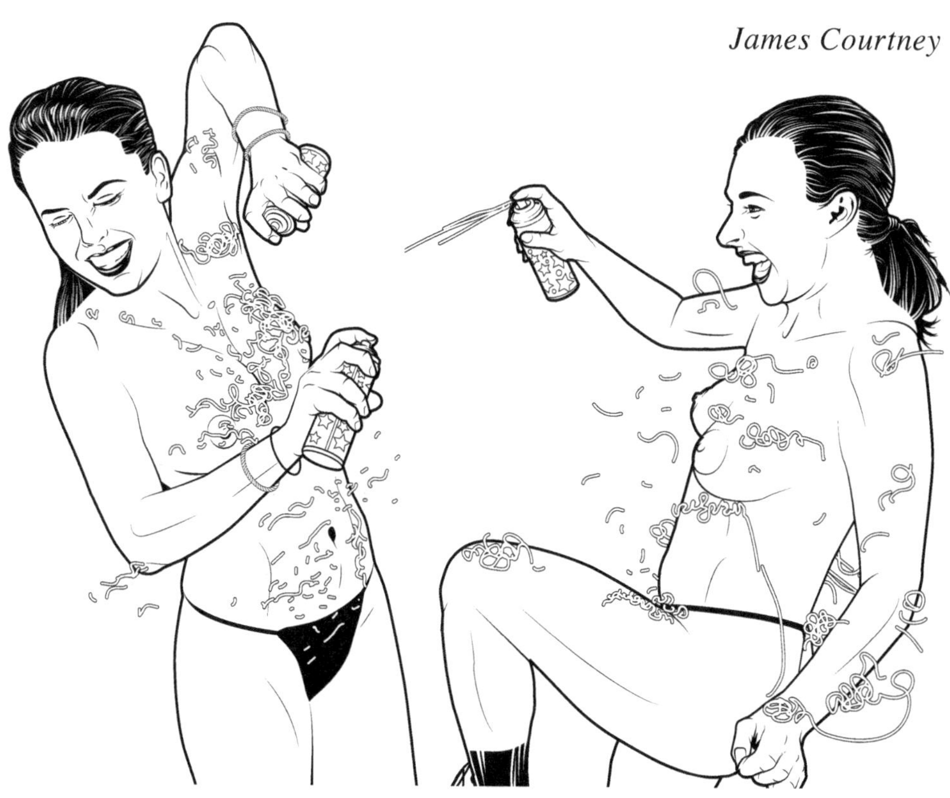

My tribute to mothers and old comic book covers. The number and date on the top refer to the first issue of Detective Comics to feature the Batman.

Bad Ass Mothers

Models: His Dame and Melissa Yvette

NO. 31 SEPTEMBER, 1939

TRUE STORIES OF BAD ASS
MOTHERS

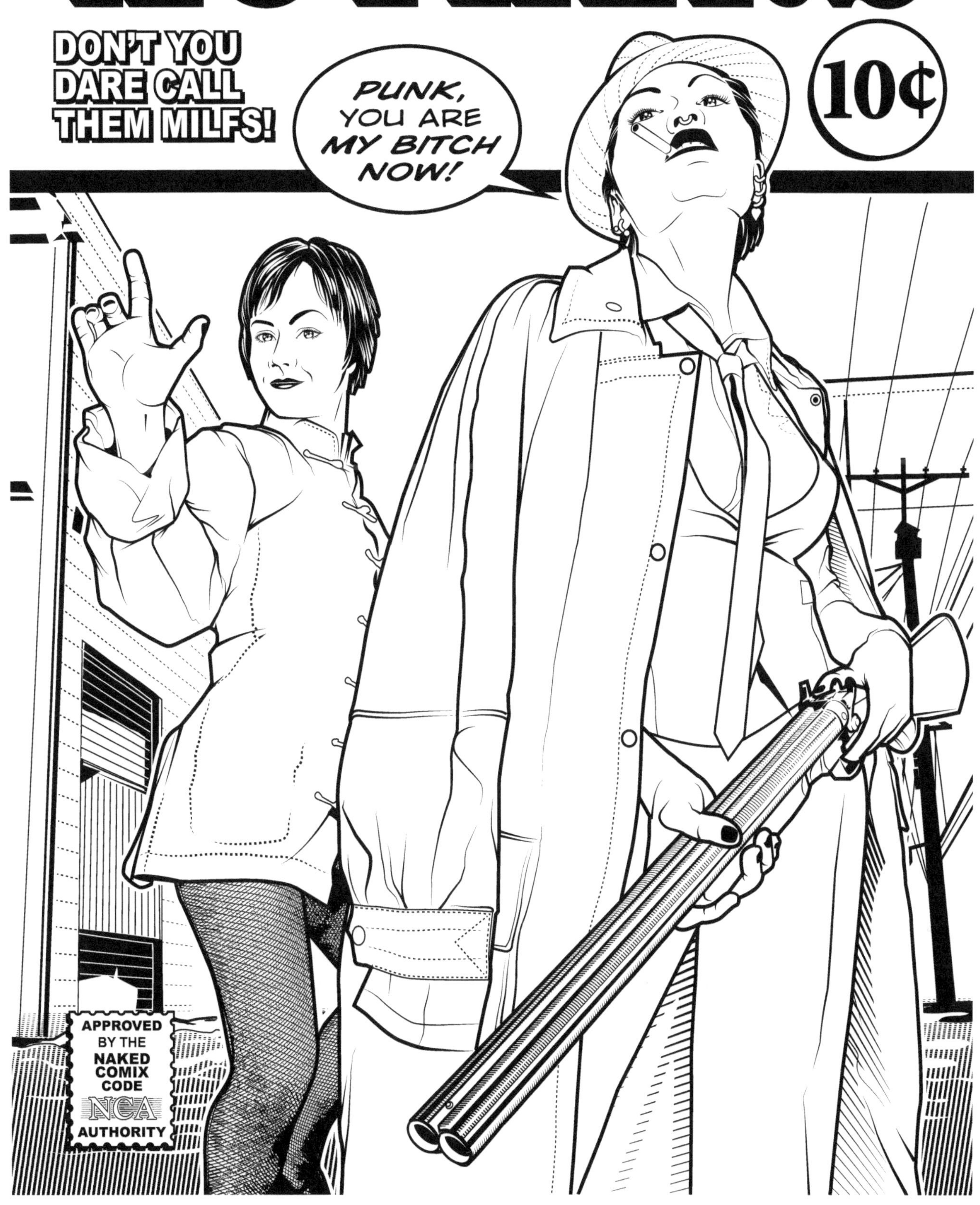

Somewhere in Gotham,
a Dark Knight hungers!

Serving The Bat

Model: Libby Loo

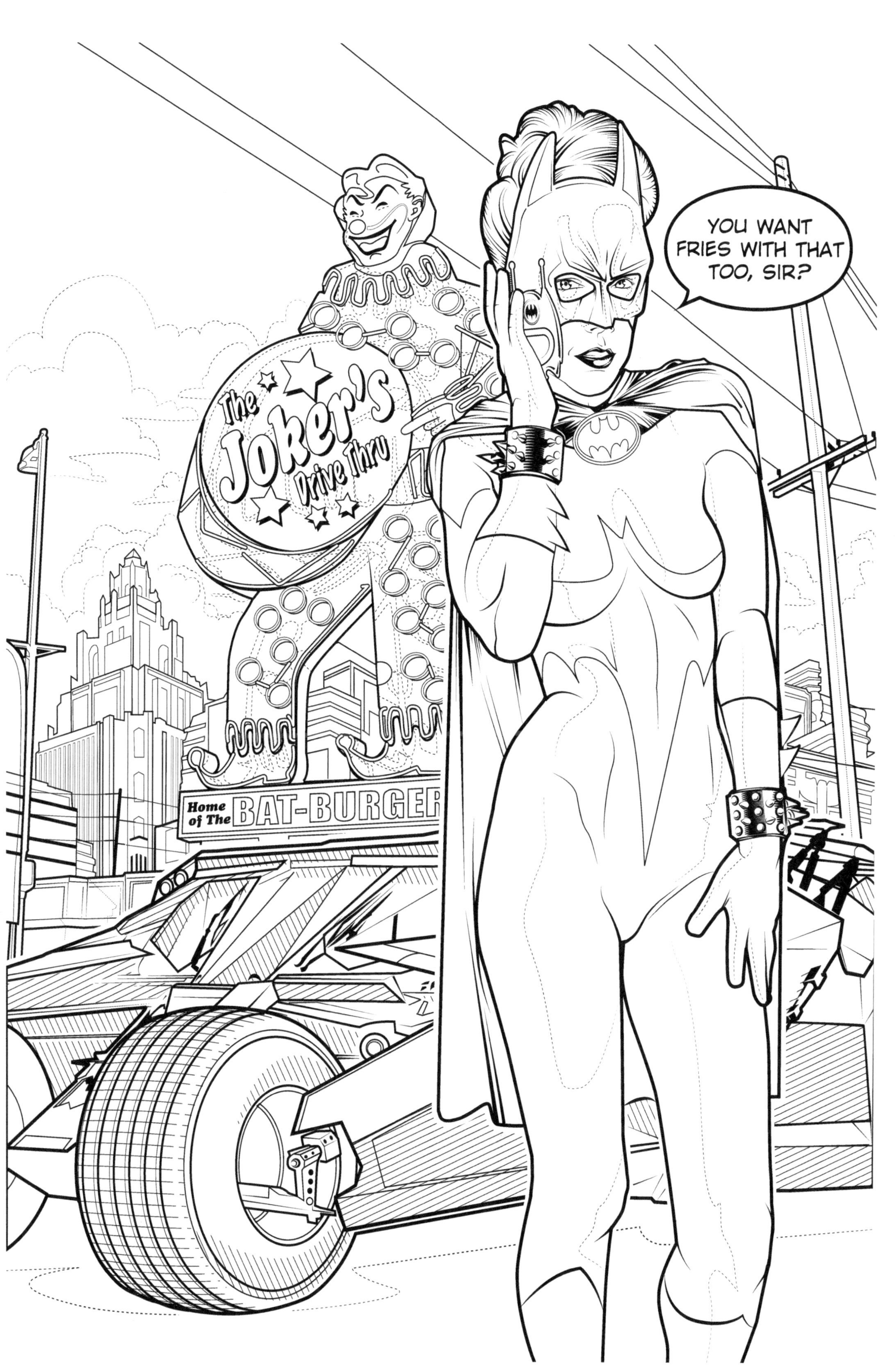
YOU WANT
FRIES WITH THAT
TOO, SIR?
The Joker's Drive Thru
Home of The BAT-BURGER

A brief glimmer into Raven Le Faye's more assertive side but don't worry Chelsea is fine by the way.

Comic Book Battles

Models: Raven Le Faye and Chelsea Christian

Special thanks to Johnny Tee Photography for the original reference image.

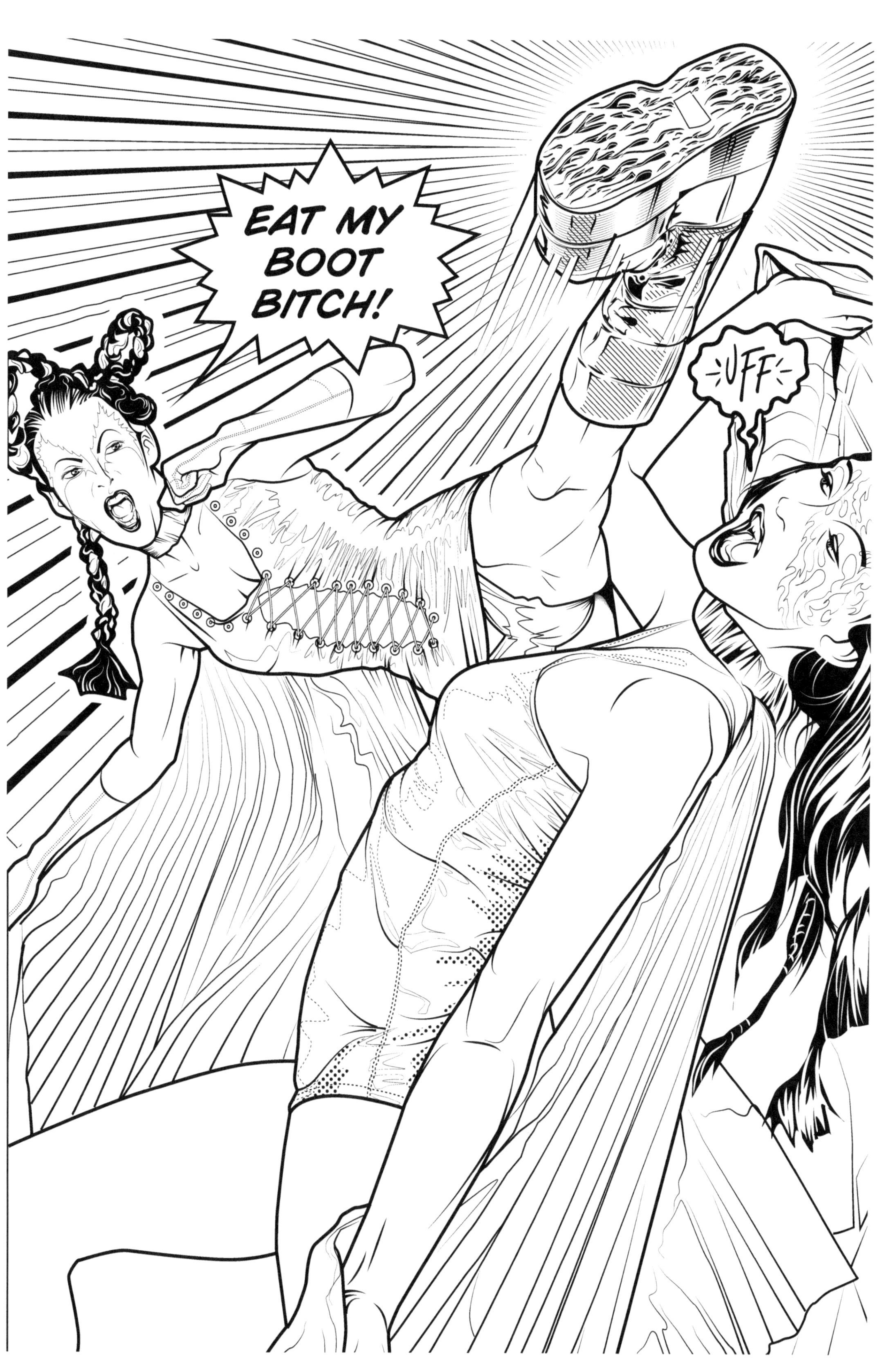
EAT MY BOOT BITCH!
UFF

Fairies: cute little mischief makers. But beware when they start bringing out the little fairy sex toys!

Bondage Fairies

Model: Eleanor R, Rigging: CorruptMorals

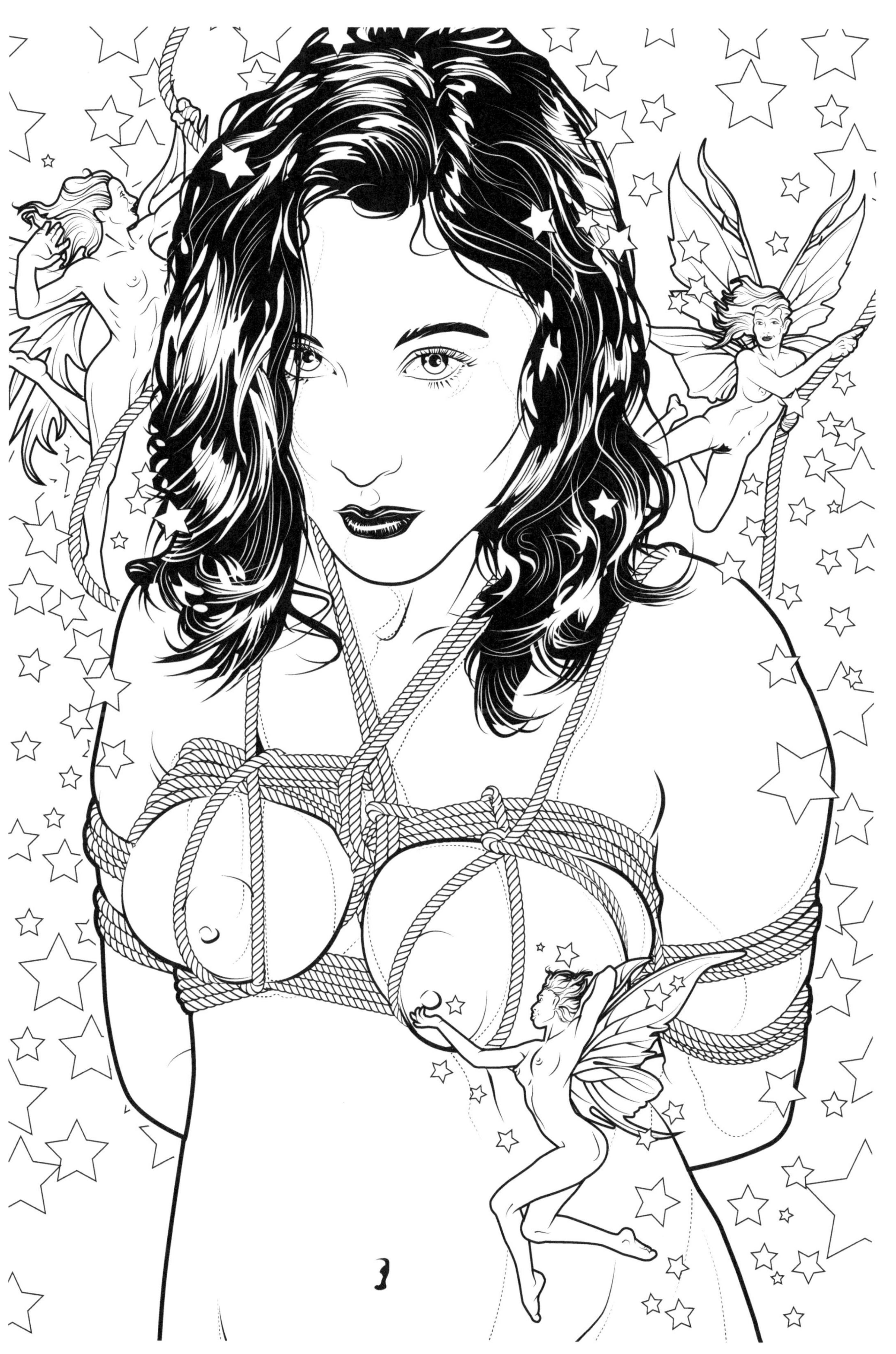

"Every Woman Is A Work Of Art
Waiting To Happen."

Bound Ballerina

Model: Raven Le Faye, Rigging: CorruptMorals

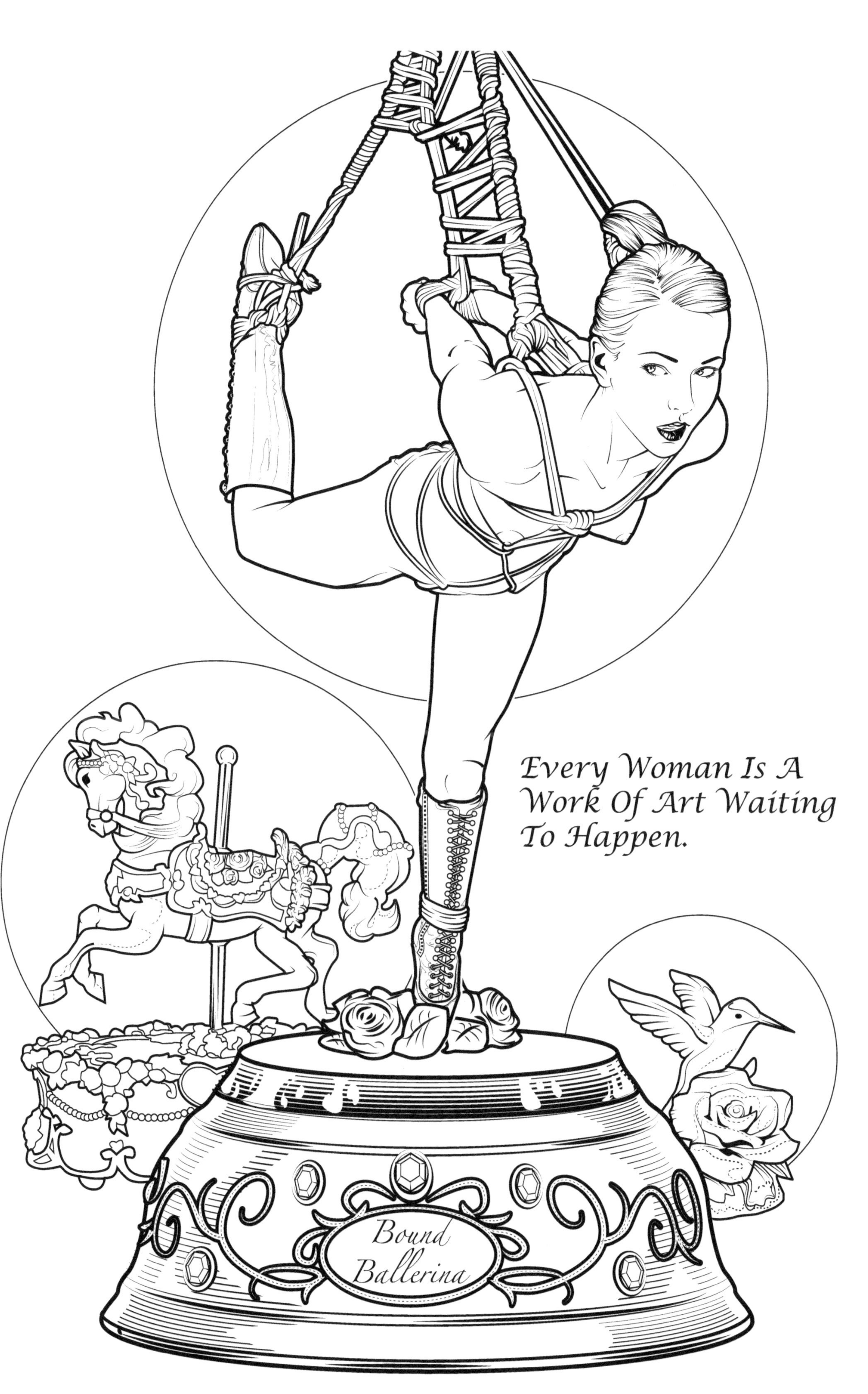
Every Woman Is A
Work Of Art Waiting
To Happen.
Bound
Ballerina

To be honest, I don't think that Mauv would actually have the rules for her submissives written in bold letters on the wall. I just added them for artistic effect. More likely, she would just carve them on their asses.

Breath Play

Models: Mauv and her boy

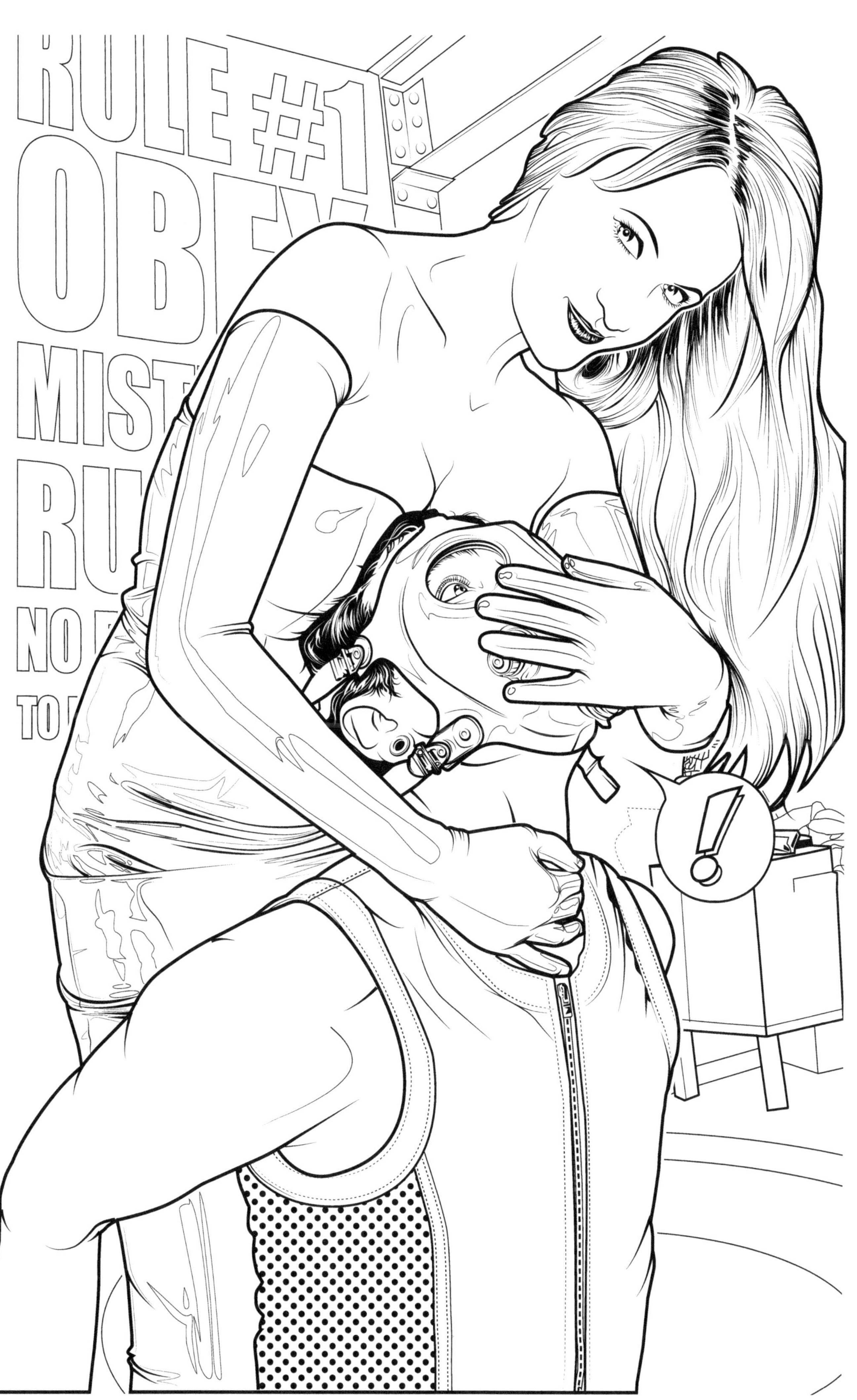
RULE #1
!

Cowgirls are like horses. You need to ride them long and hard, and bring them back to the barn sweaty and satisfied!

Cowgirls

Models: Melisande and Penny McClish

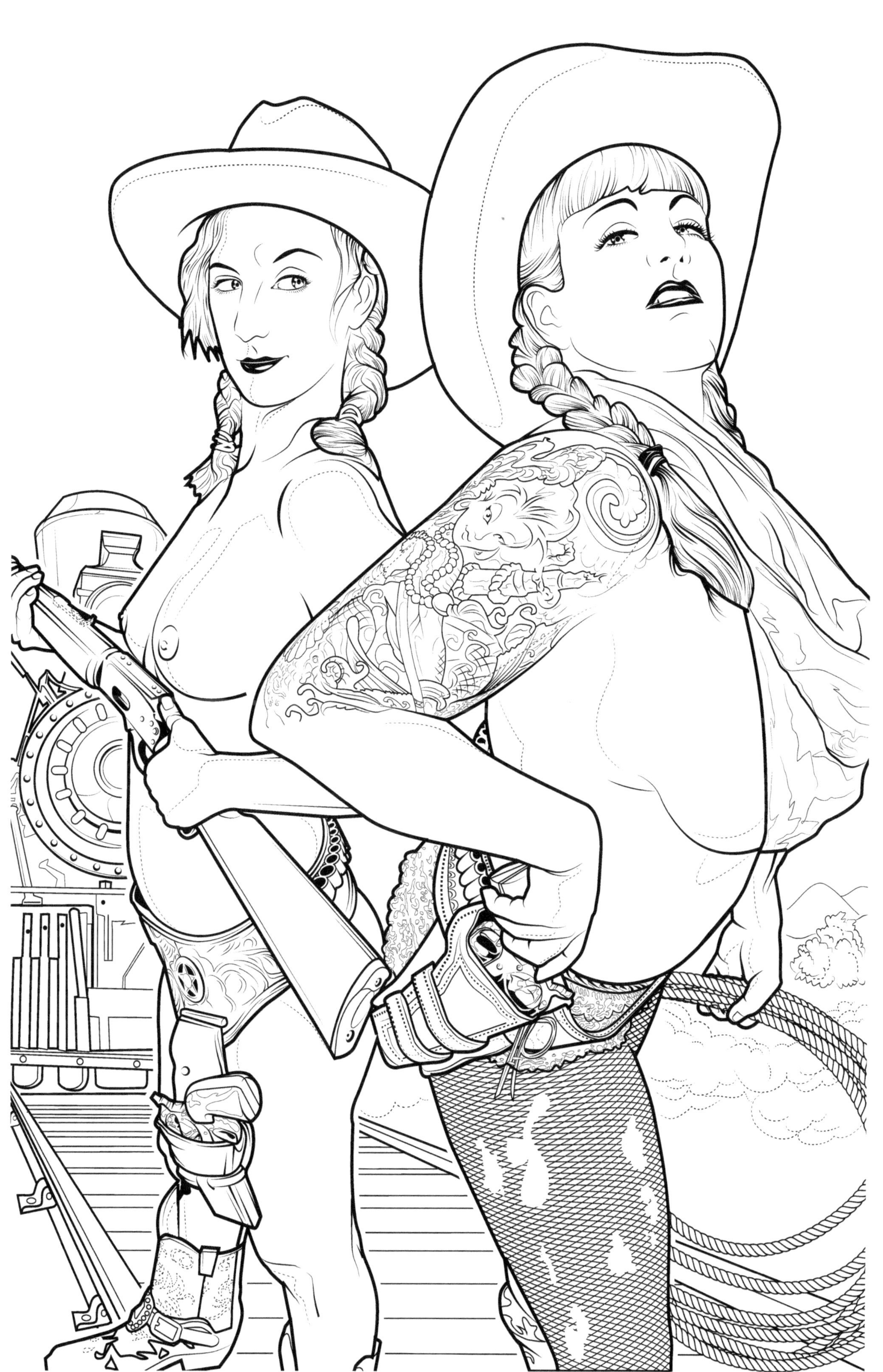

Jim Higgins supplied the "naked motorcycle" for this picture. He explained to me that there was once a famous motorcyclist who would actually surf like this on his motorcycle. That is, until he fell off and died. So kids, don't try this at home!

Cycle Surfing

Model: Dizzy Night

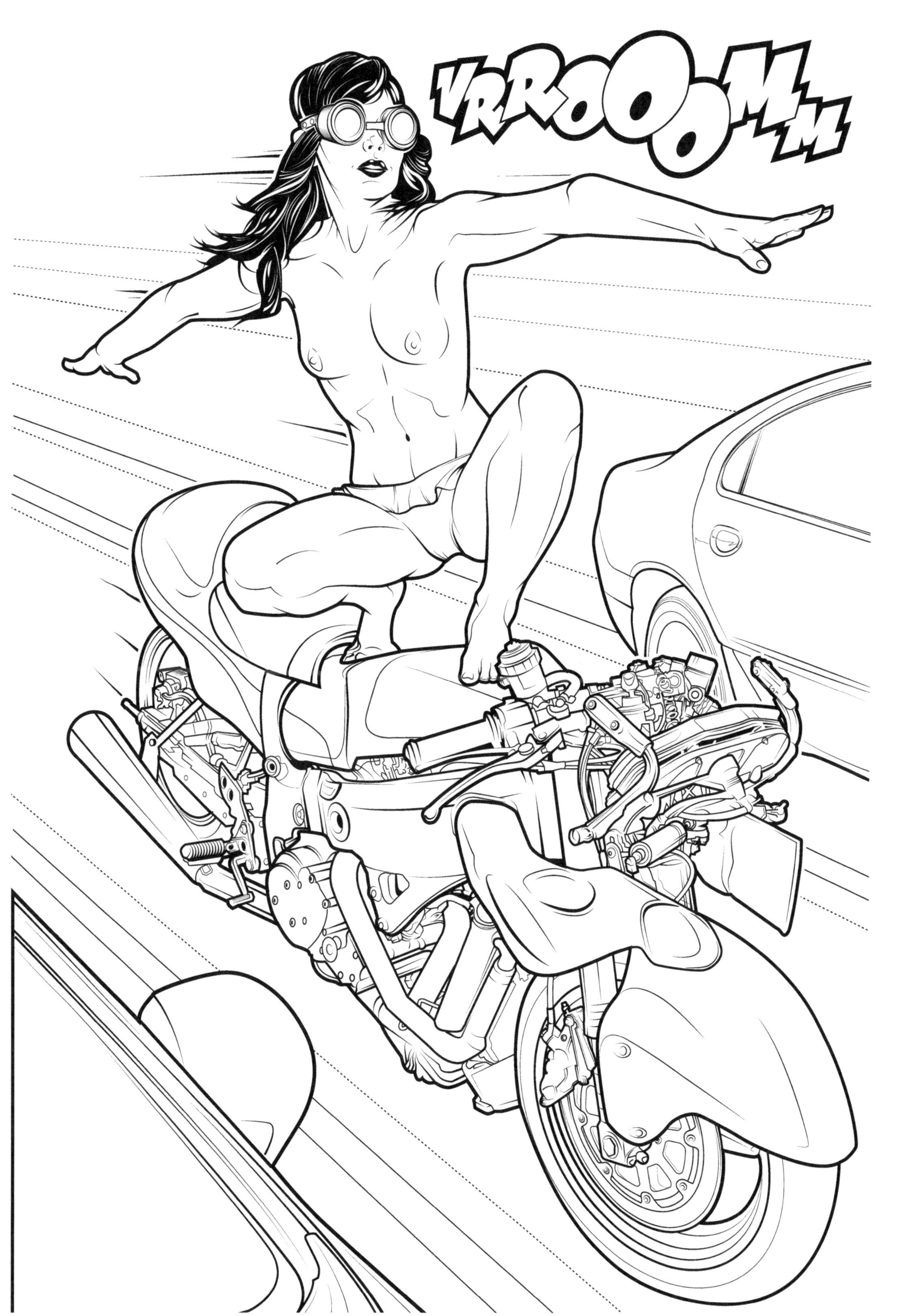
VRROOOMM

I'm happy with how this turned out. I always love the chance to draw smoke like Alphonse Mucha. I wonder, though, what it means that the most sexually suggestive part of the image is the ashtray?

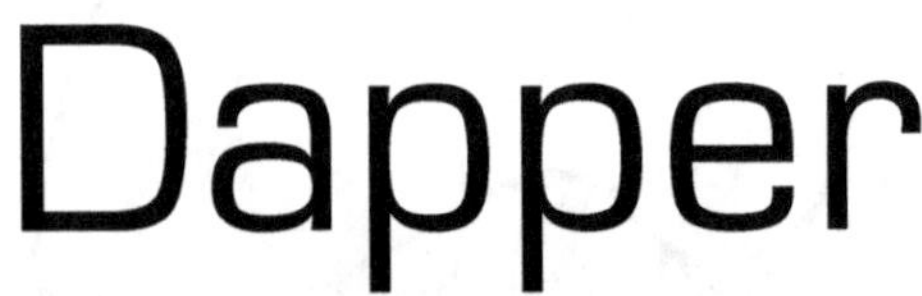

Model: Skittles88

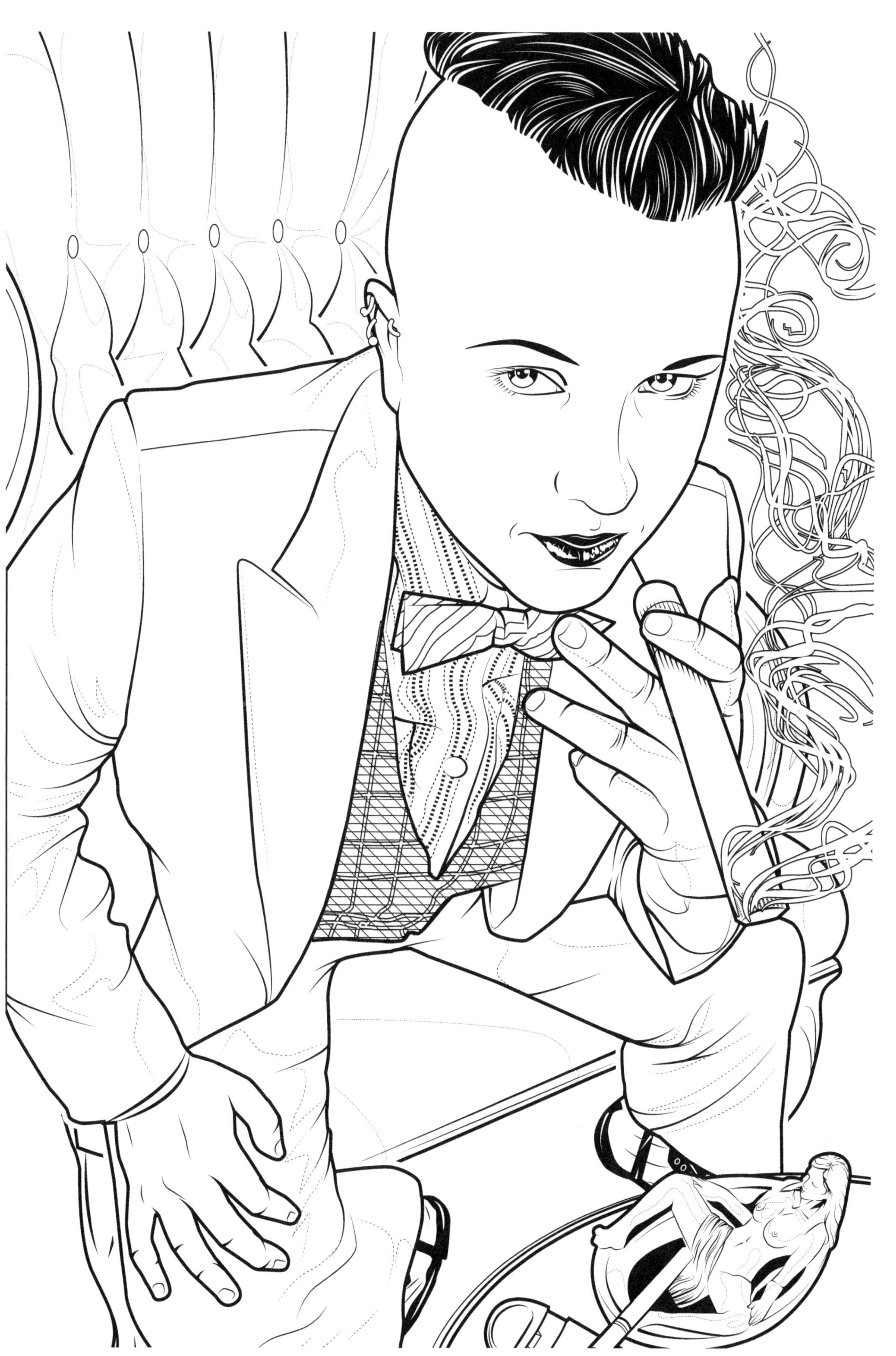

Given the amount of detail in the image, this picture seemed to take forever. But you can't really have a coloring book unless you give people things to draw. I have had a few people compliment me on the subtle D/S vibe running through the reference photo for this picture. Though I tend to favor images of strong, assertive women, do not take that to mean I don't have the utmost respect to those men and women working in service positions.

The Client Is Waiting

Models: Jeff Cathcart and Arcadia Kane

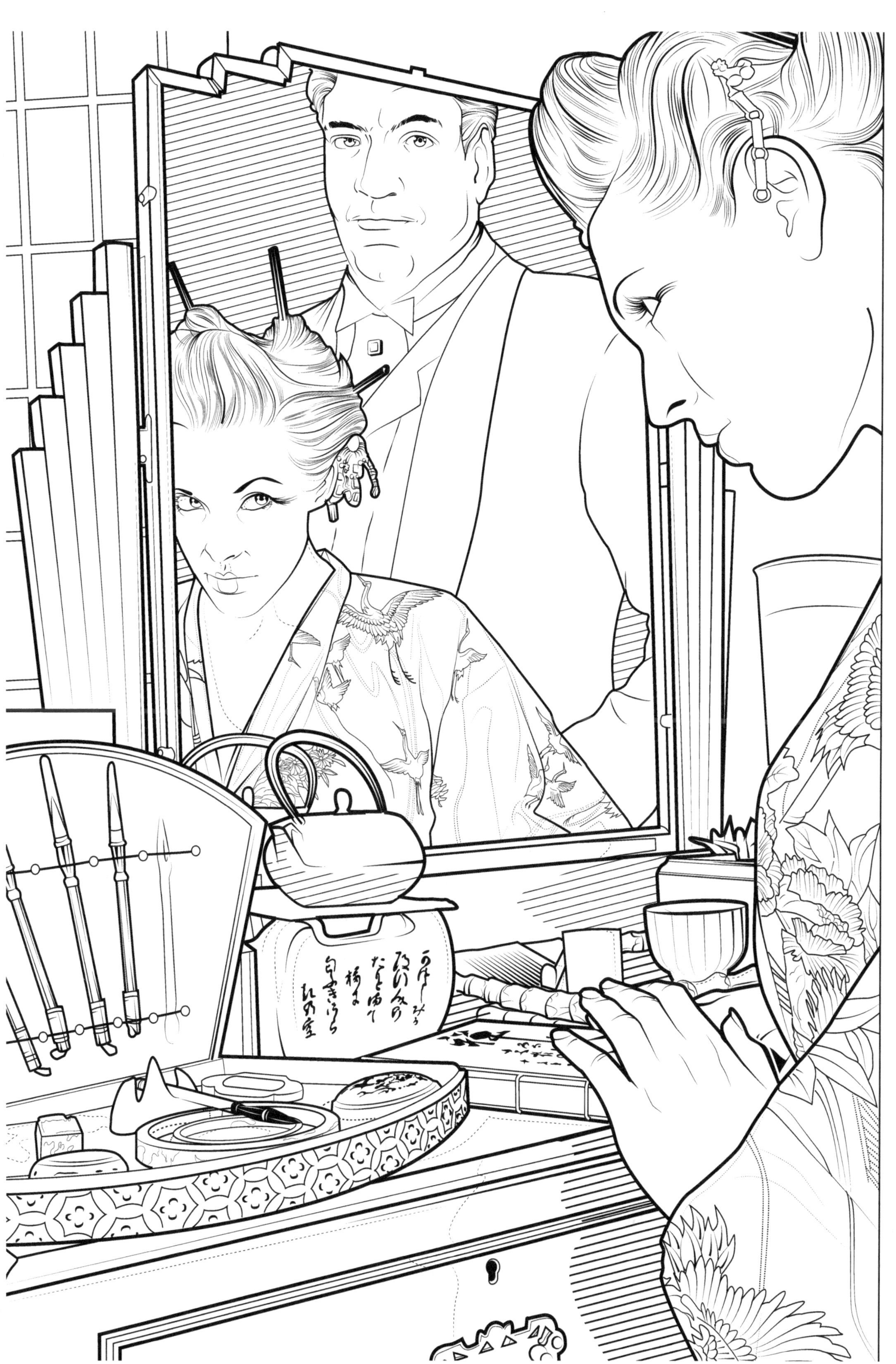

While I was drawing this, it really felt like Skittles88 needed a tattoo on her arm. So when I asked her what type of tattoo she would like, she said a Chinese Dragon since she was born in the Year of the Dragon. People born on the Year of the Dragon are supposed to be vigorous, strong, self-assured, proud and passionate. I guess the woman on the bed is supposed to show what happens to you when you sleep with a dragon.

Girl With The Dragon Tattoo

Model: Skittles88

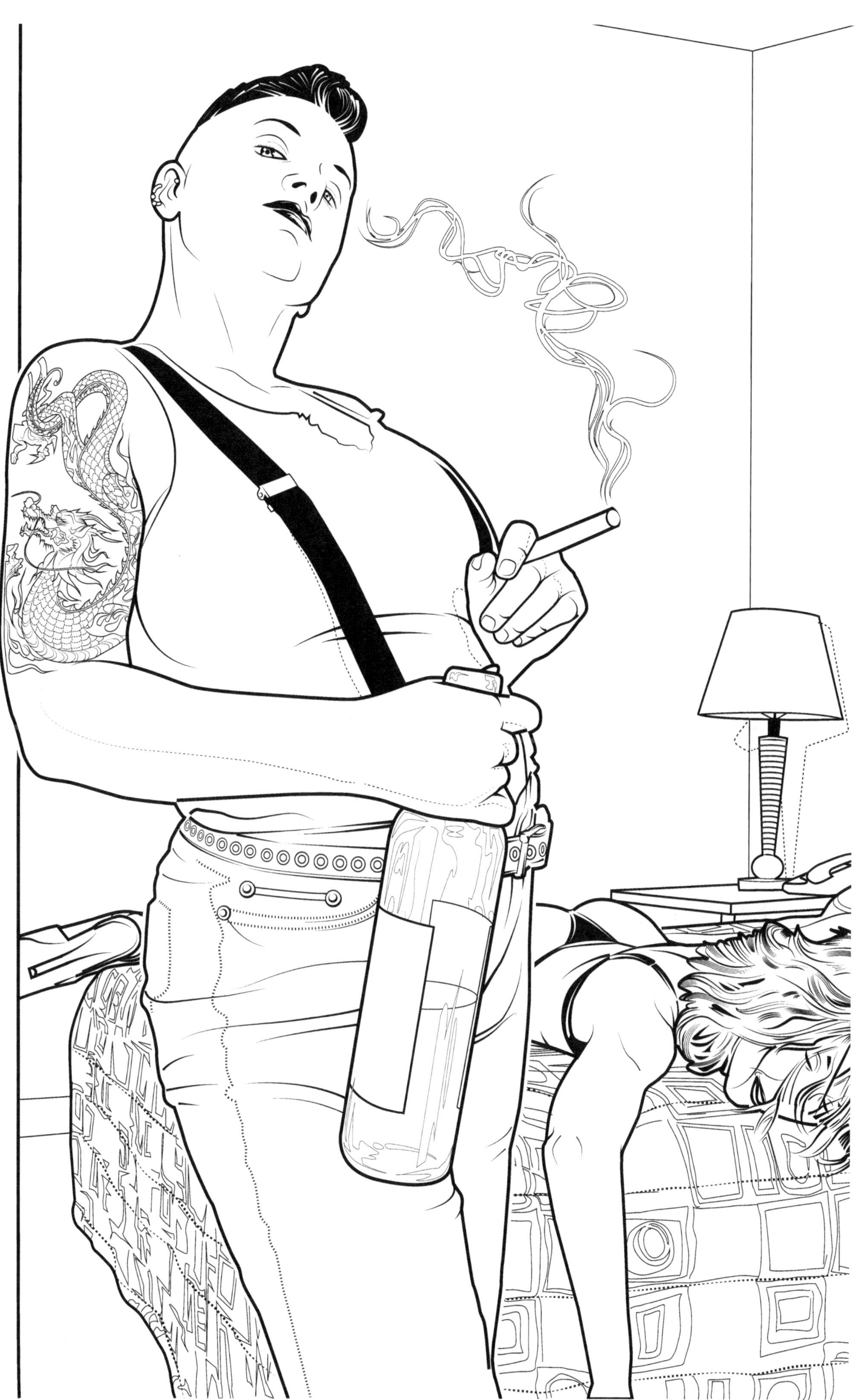

There has been one criticism about the Kinky Coloring Books that I have been trying to address: the need for more guys in it. I don't know if I will ever be able to go make an all male coloring book but I can at least try and be more "heteroflexible" in the subject matter choices in this one.

Go-Go Guys

Location: 2013 Folsom Street Fair San Francisco

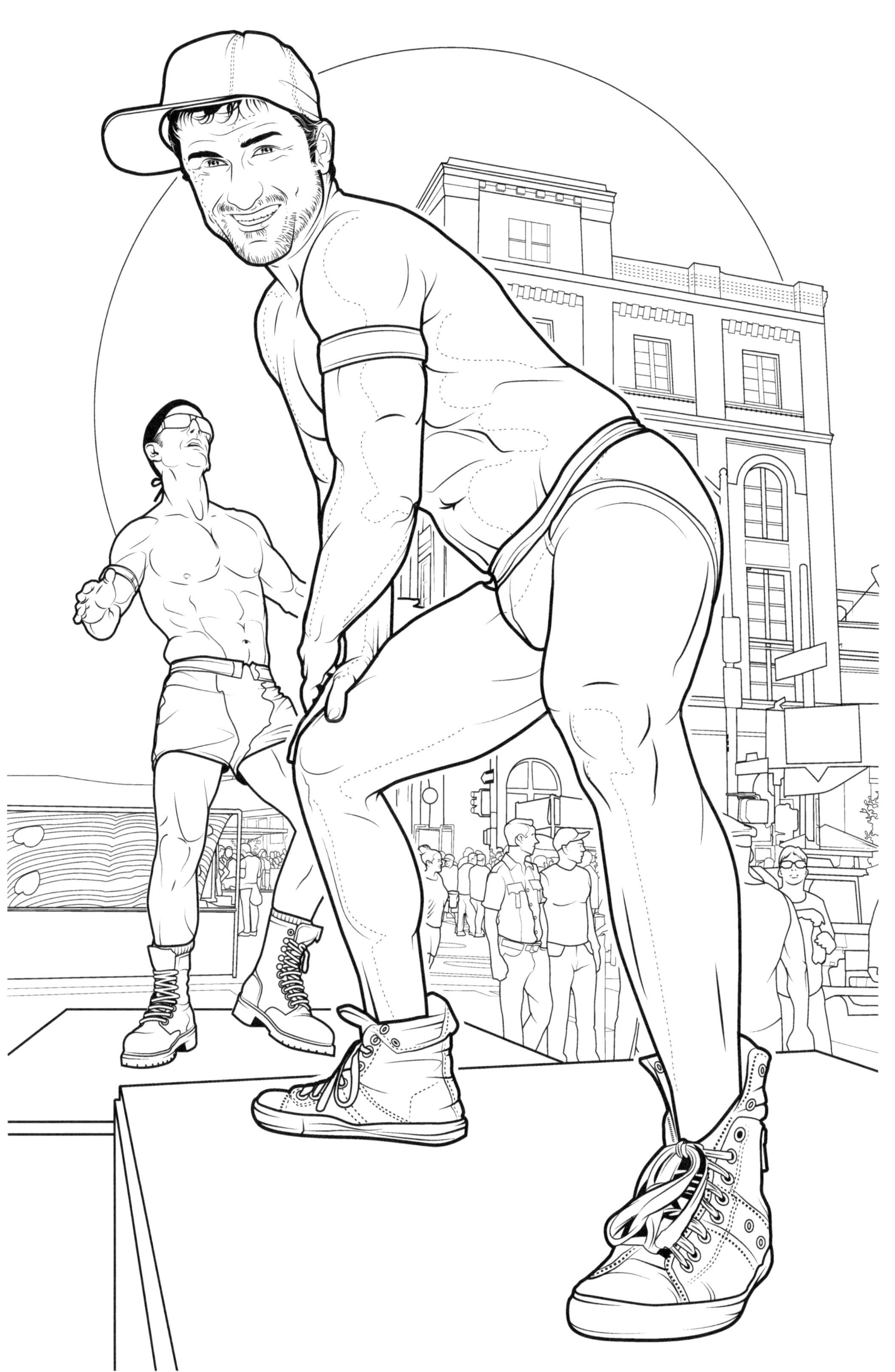

The whole idea of hair pulling seems to be the one thing that is universal among the D/S players. For tops, there is a certain pleasure in just grabbing hold and asserting your control. For bottoms, it seems like something that puts most in a submissive state right away. Even the reverse seems popular among many. I have noticed a few doms enjoying getting their hair combed and brushed by their subs.

Hair Pull

Models: CorruptMorals and HisDame

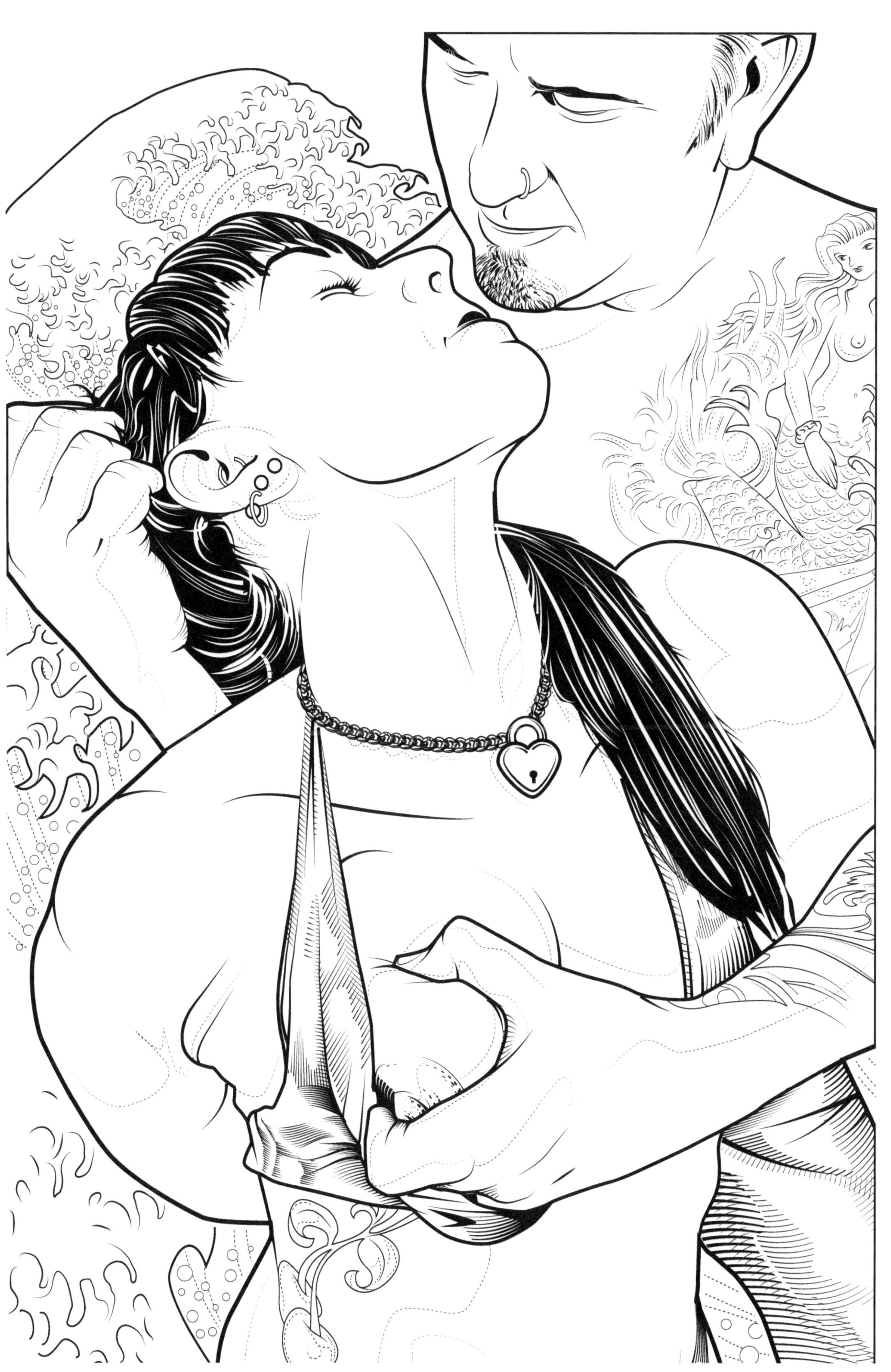

I finished this within 24 hours of starting. That is something that rarely happens with me. I usually do my illustrations over the course of a couple of days, just putting in an hour at a time. But work was hell and my home life was getting stressful too, I needed a mental break. So Saturday night and Sunday morning, I sat down at my computer and just banged it out. I felt better when it was done. I guess I really needed some happy clown time.

Happy Clown

Model: Stripes The Clown

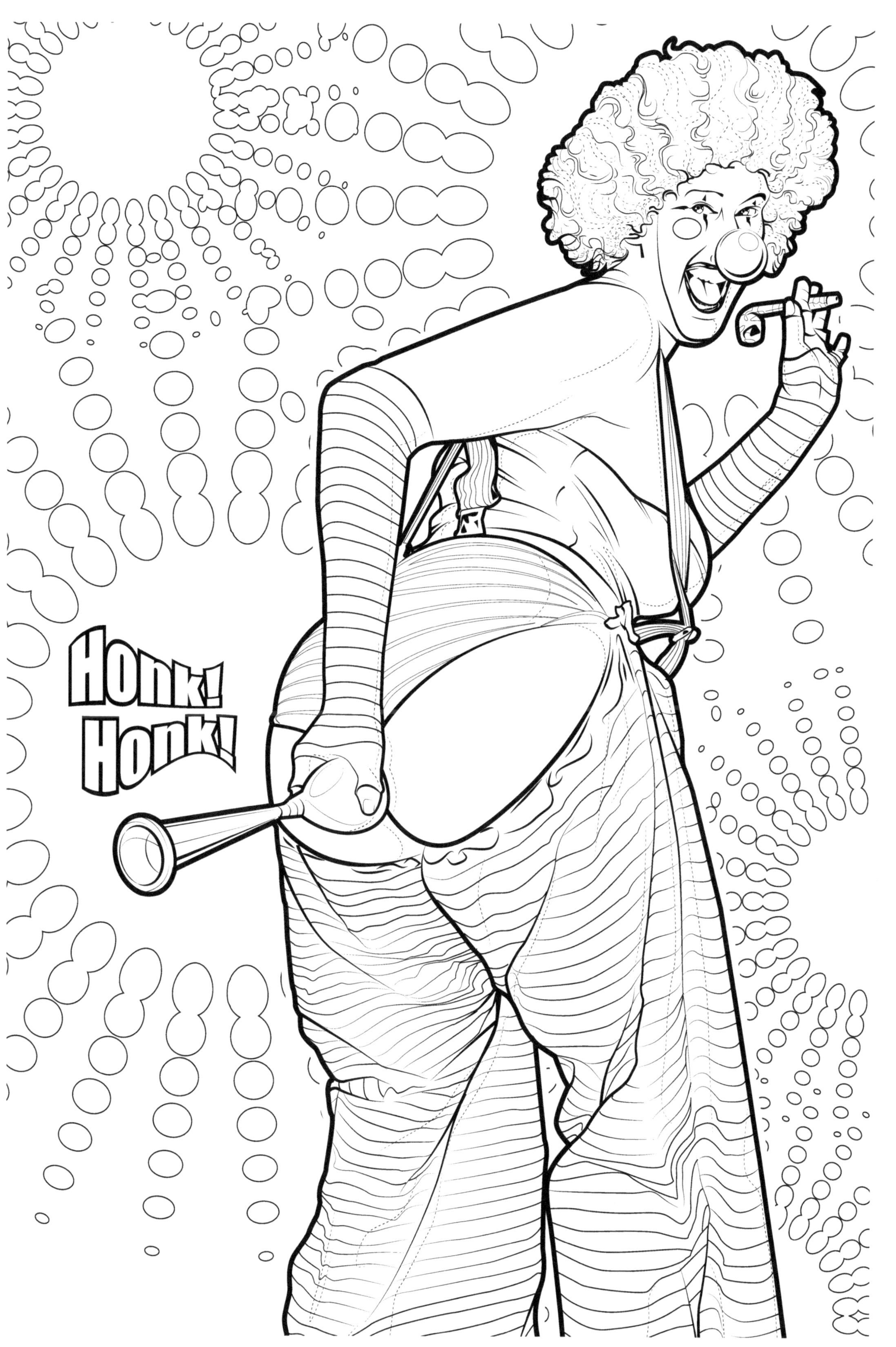
Honk!
Honk!

What is Raven thinking? I haven't a clue,
but I'm sure it is interesting.

Iron Raven

Model: Raven Le faye

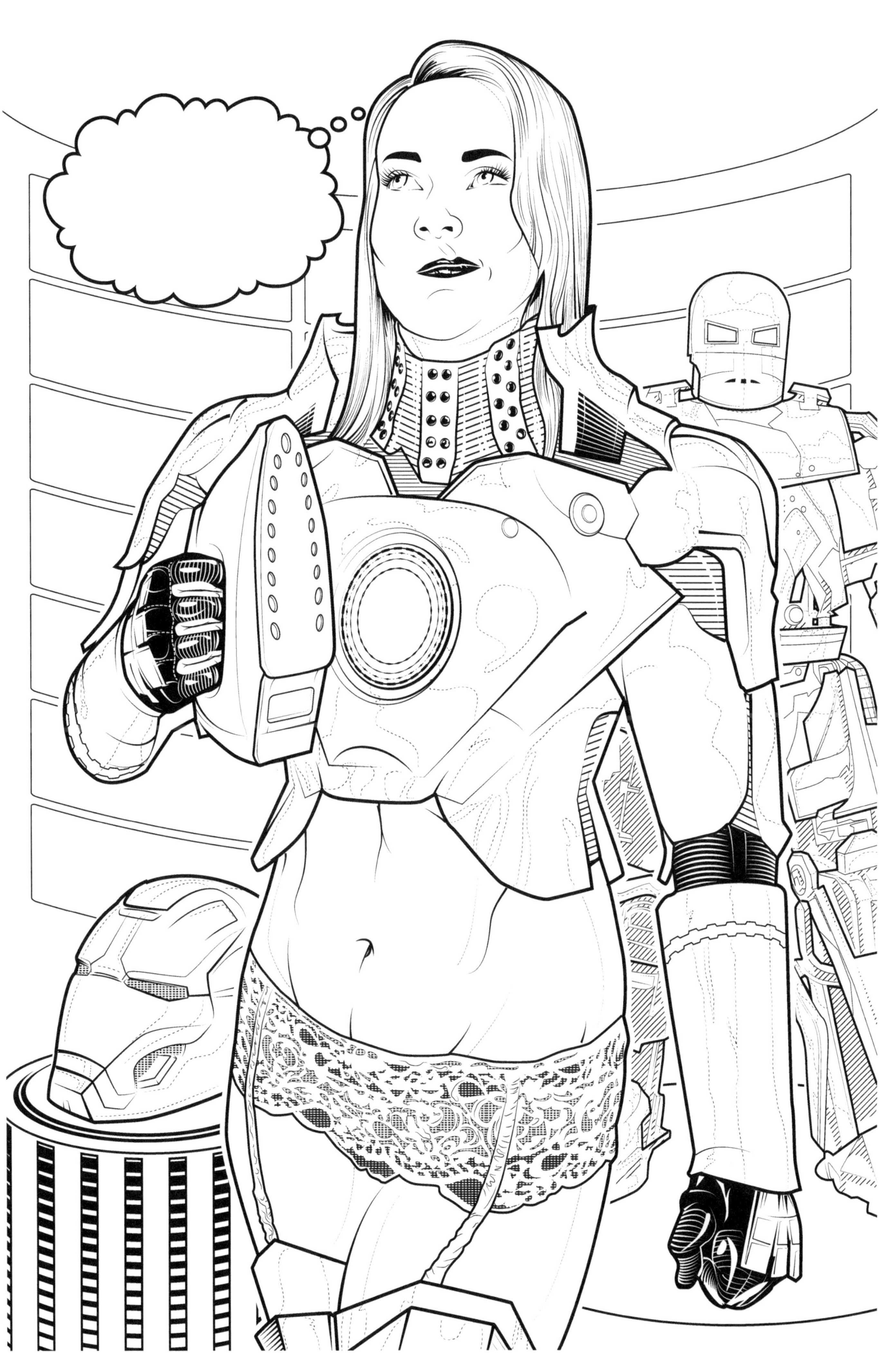

How many licks does it take to get to the center?

Lick it

Model: Davina Darling and "Loaflette"

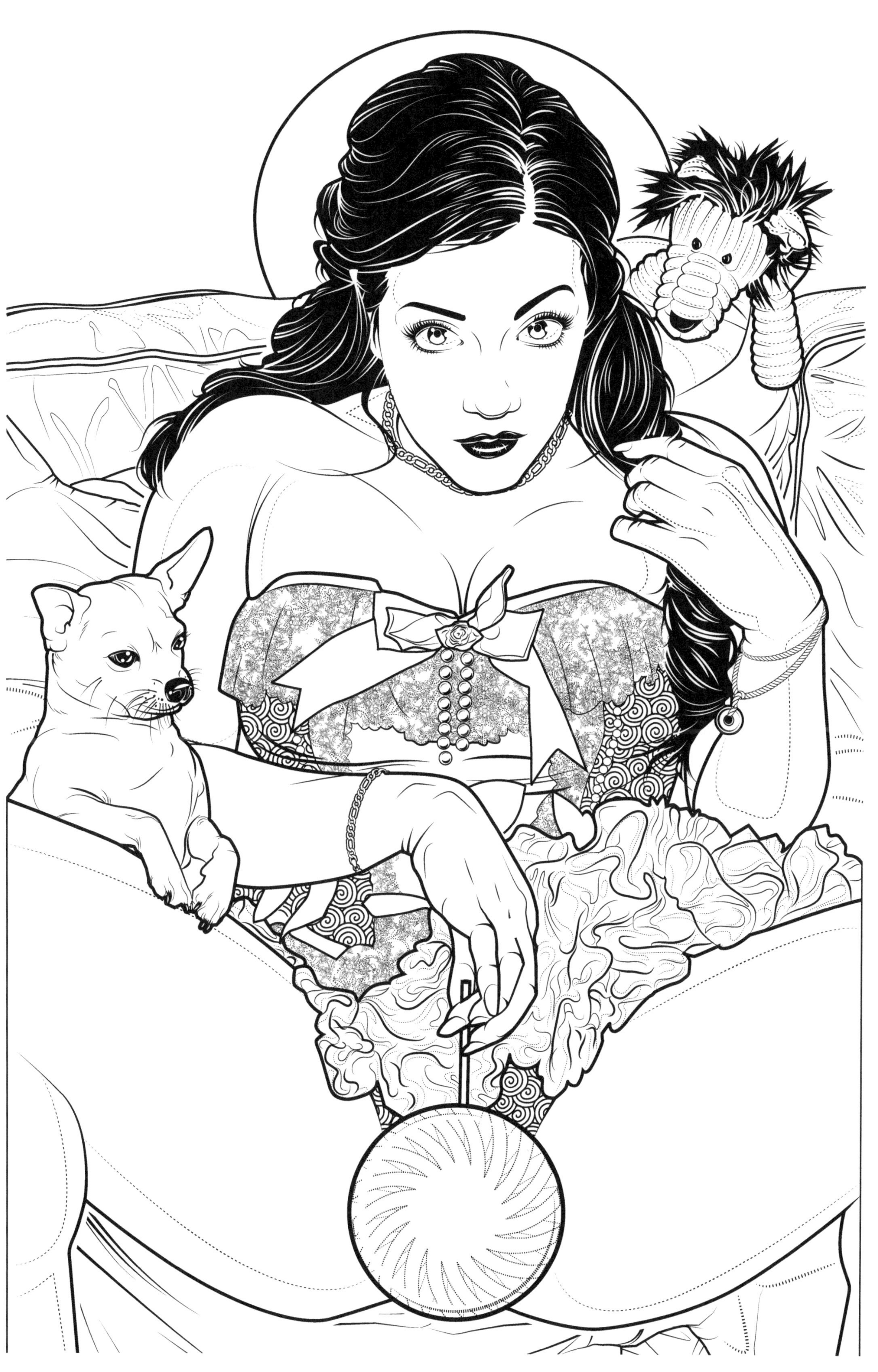

Little Davina would like to read a story to you, and she guarantees it will have a happy ending.

Little Davina

Model: Davina Darling

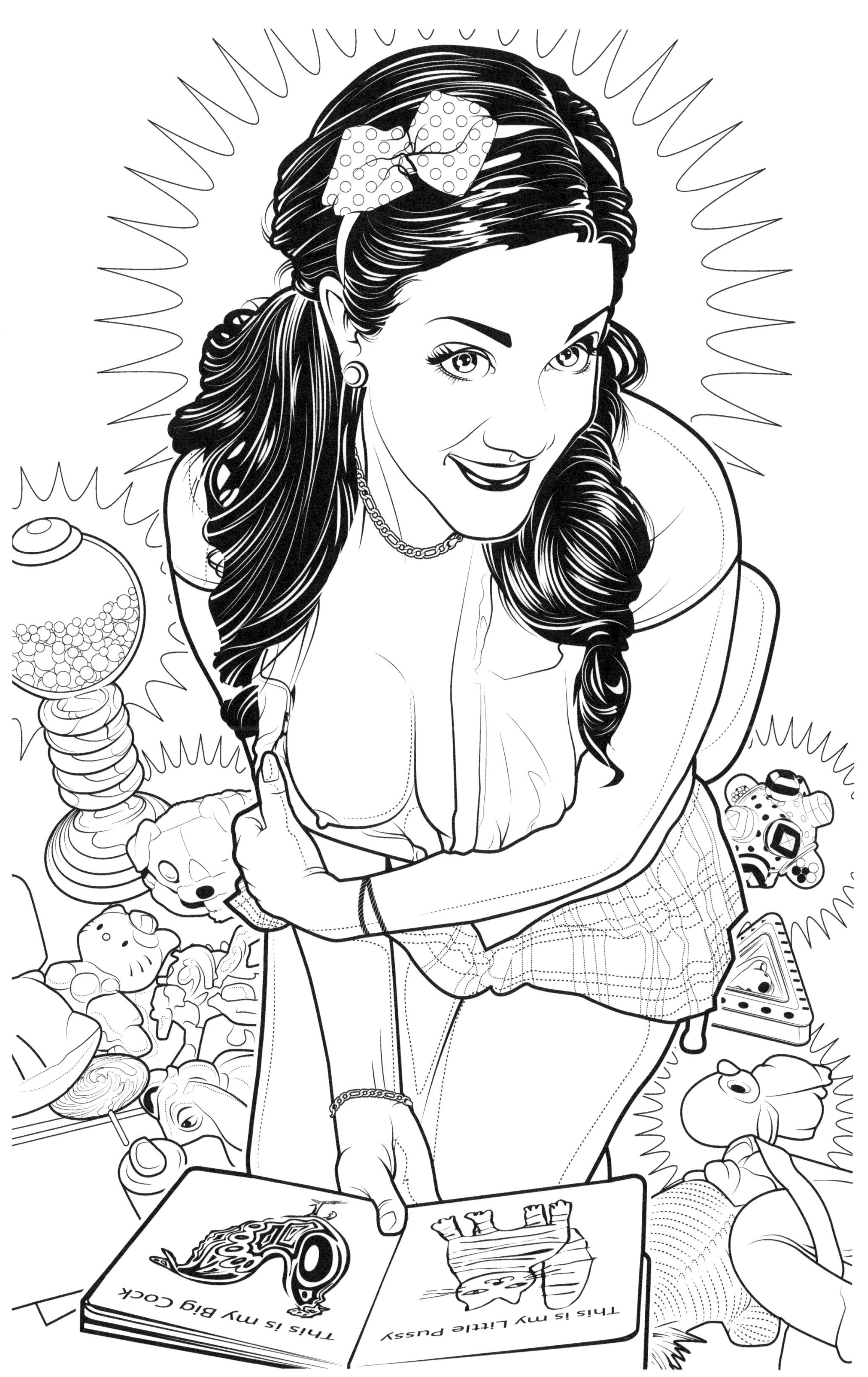
This is my Big Cock
This is my Little Pussy

Some days Mommy needs just a little help
to keep those brats in line.

Mommy's Little Helper

Models: Jessie Marie and Roxxie

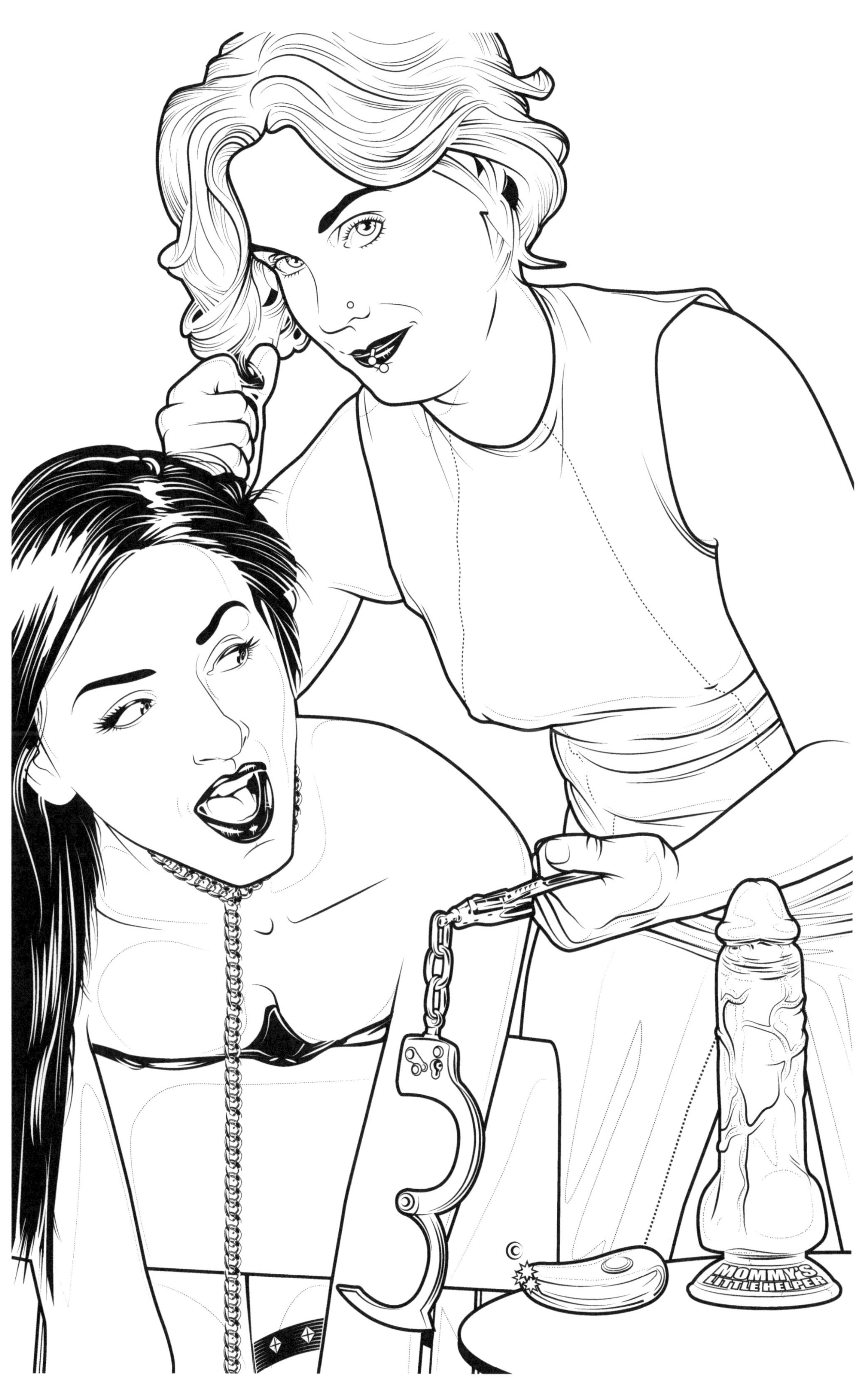
©
MOMMY'S
LITTLE HELPER

In the end, naughty girls always get spanked.

Morning After Mark

Model: Courtney Cass

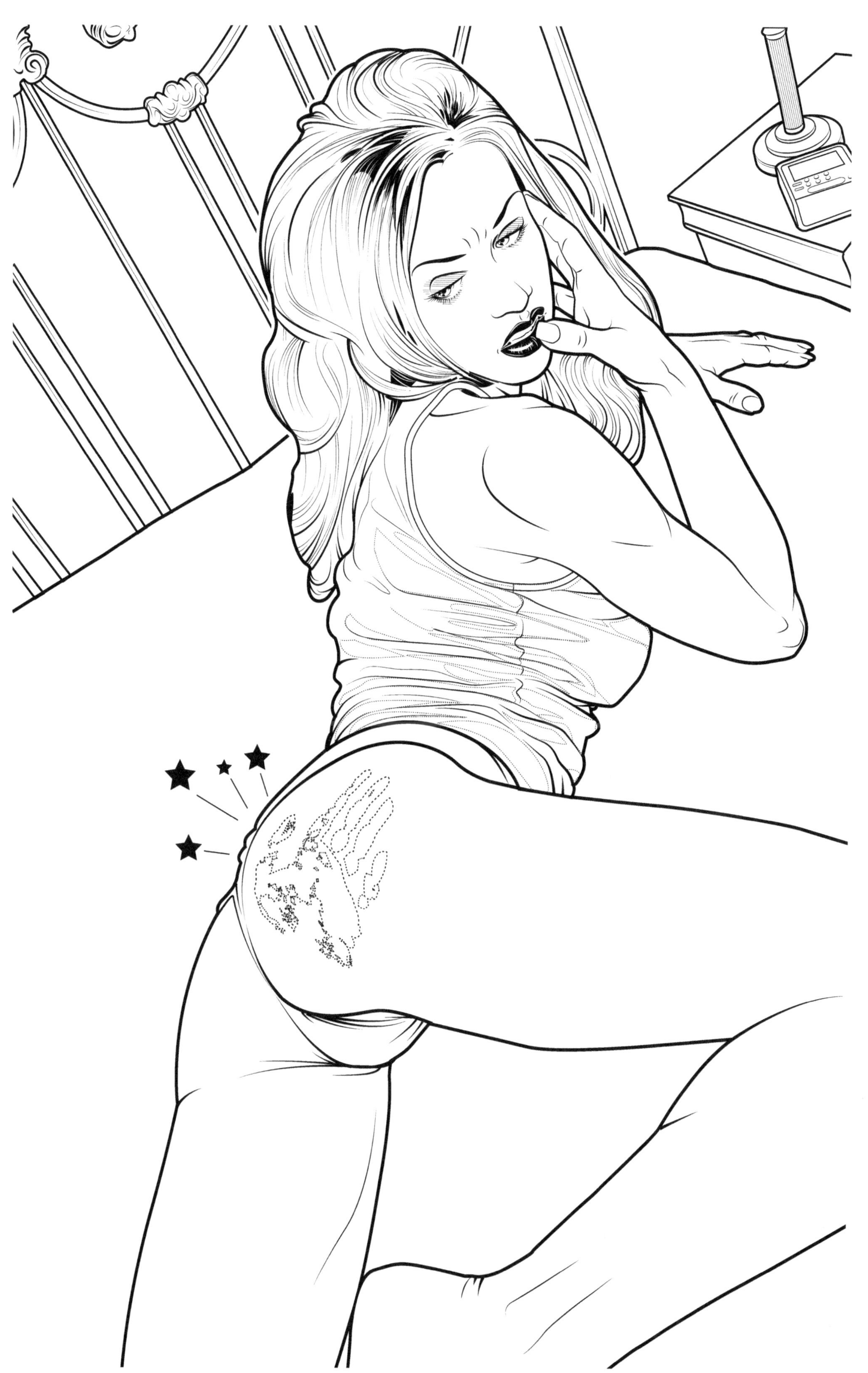

For the record, I want people to know that Eastbaysinner510 is actually a pretty cool dude. But as an expert needle top, I've seen many a lady line up to be a part of his sadistic artistry. Proving you can be quite popular being a "prick" to women.

What A Prick!

Models: Eastbaysinner510 and Purrplexitty
Hair: Justina Downs
Needles: Eastbaysinner510

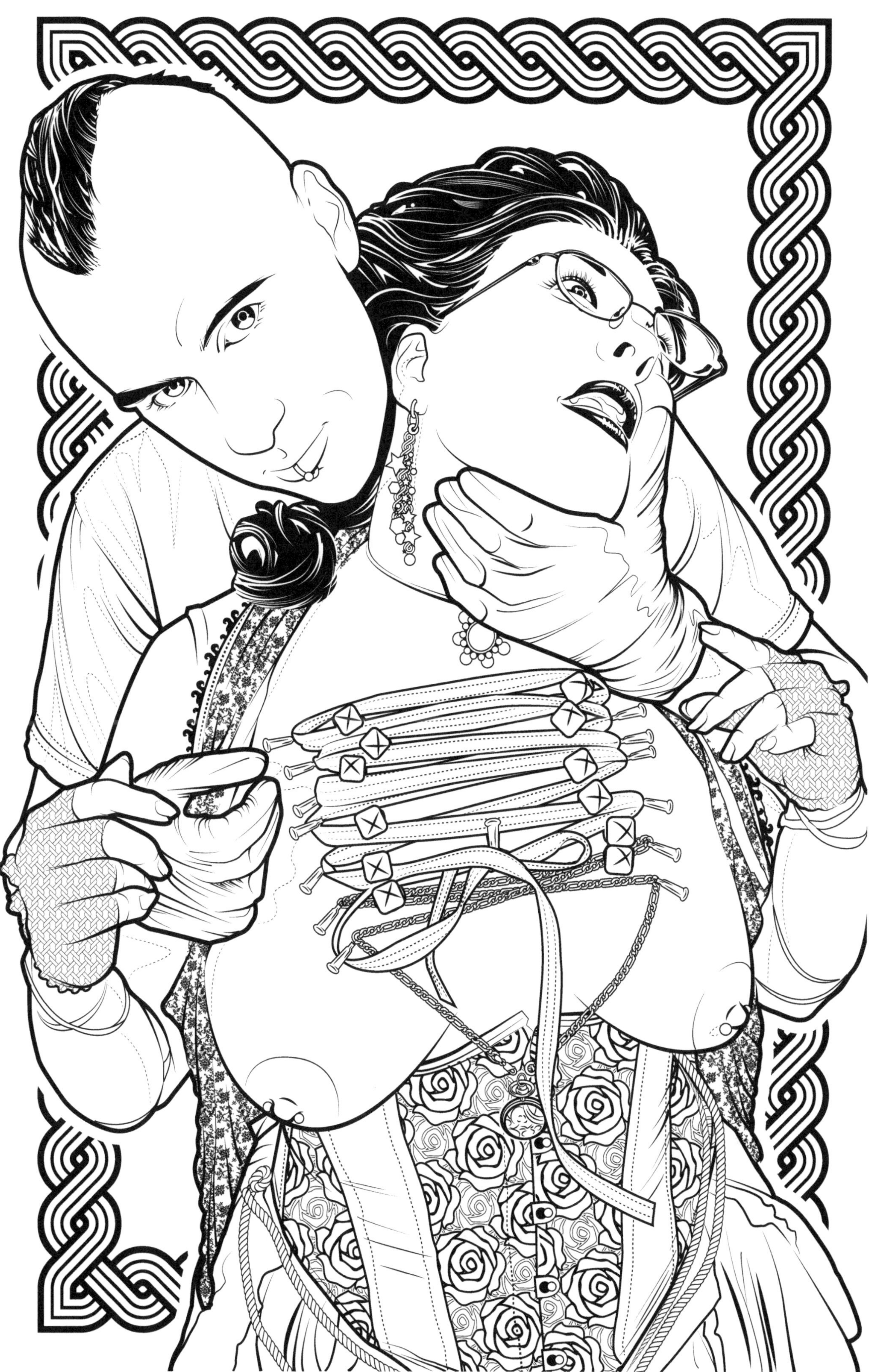

The reference photo for this illustration was shot way back in 2007 at a photography workshop put on by Charles Gatewood at the old SF Citadel. Surprisingly, this is the only the second illustration I have ever done from that set. I think at the time, I wasn't ready to take on fetish themes. Now this almost feels too tame.

Playtime

Models: Sade Luna and Dragon Sundancer

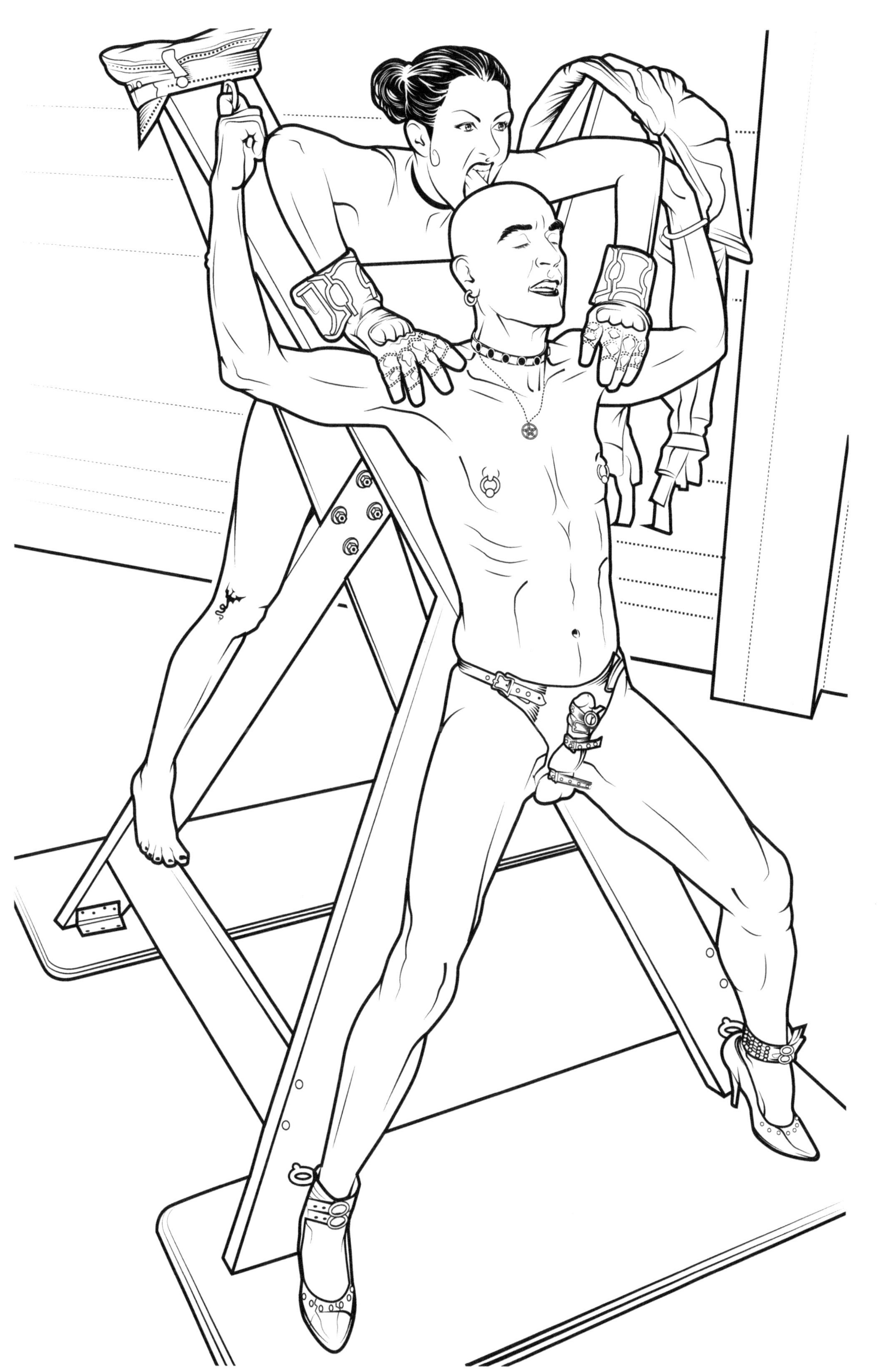

The reference photo for this drawing was one I took back in 2006 of the amazing Rasa Vitalia (www.rasavitalia.com). The guitar she is holding is a limited edition Stevie Ray Vaughn signature Fender Stratocaster owned by my cousin Robert Jordan. Robert is a established East Bay musician and Rasa is a well known Bay Area dancer and singer. I'm lucky to be surrounded by such talented family and friends.

Ready To Rock

Model: Rasa Vitalia

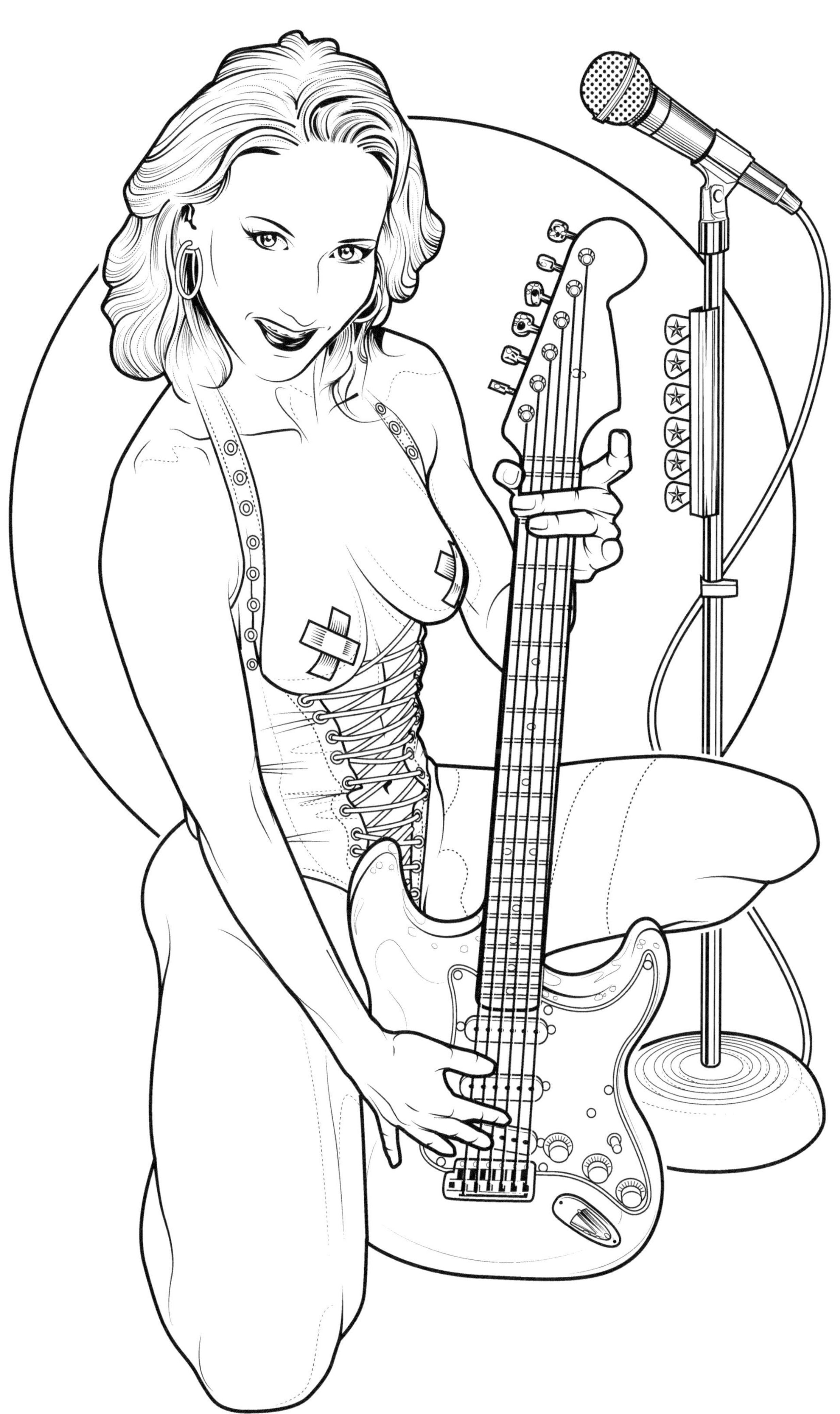

At Hogwarts, Gryffindor has the heroes, Hufflepuff the builders and Ravenclaw the brains. But it is always House Slytherin that has the best looking babes!

Slytherin Babe

Model: Chelsea Christian

Latex Dress Designed by Penny McClish of Lust Designs

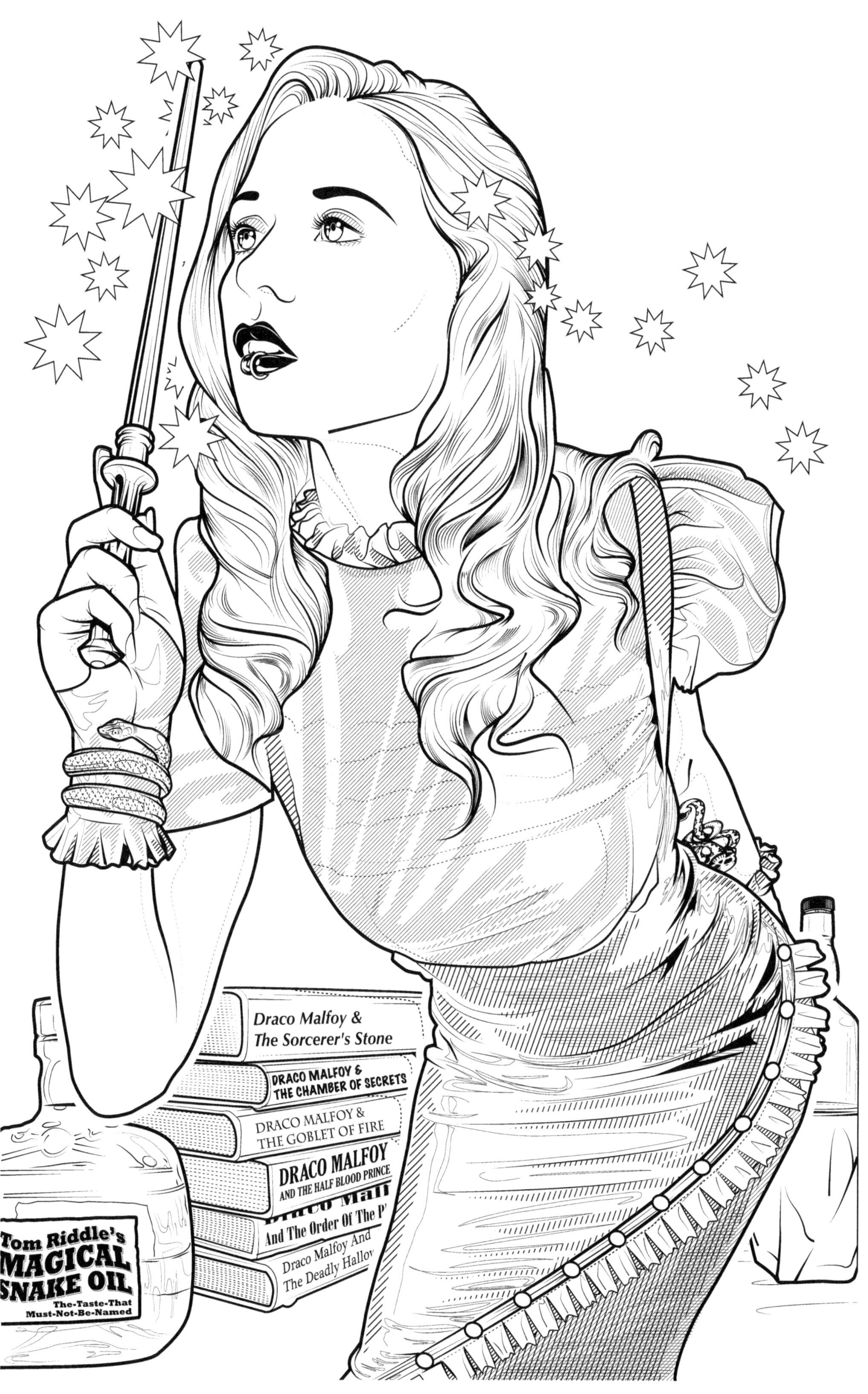
Draco Malfoy &
The Sorcerer's Stone
DRACO MALFOY &
THE CHAMBER OF SECRETS
DRACO MALFOY &
THE GOBLET OF FIRE
DRACO MALFOY
AND THE HALF BLOOD PRINCE
And The Order Of The
Draco Malfoy And
The Deadly
Tom Riddle's
MAGICAL
SNAKE OIL
The-Taste-That
Must-Not-Be-Named

After watching a whole season of "InkMaster", I felt compelled to do a "tattoo-centric" illustration for the next Kinky Coloring Book. A tattoo artist herself, I felt that Basia would be the perfect candidate for this. This was a safe way to exorcize any desire to go under the needle myself. I would be the worst tattoo client ever. I hate pain, needles and bad design equally.

Tattooed Basia

Model: Basia

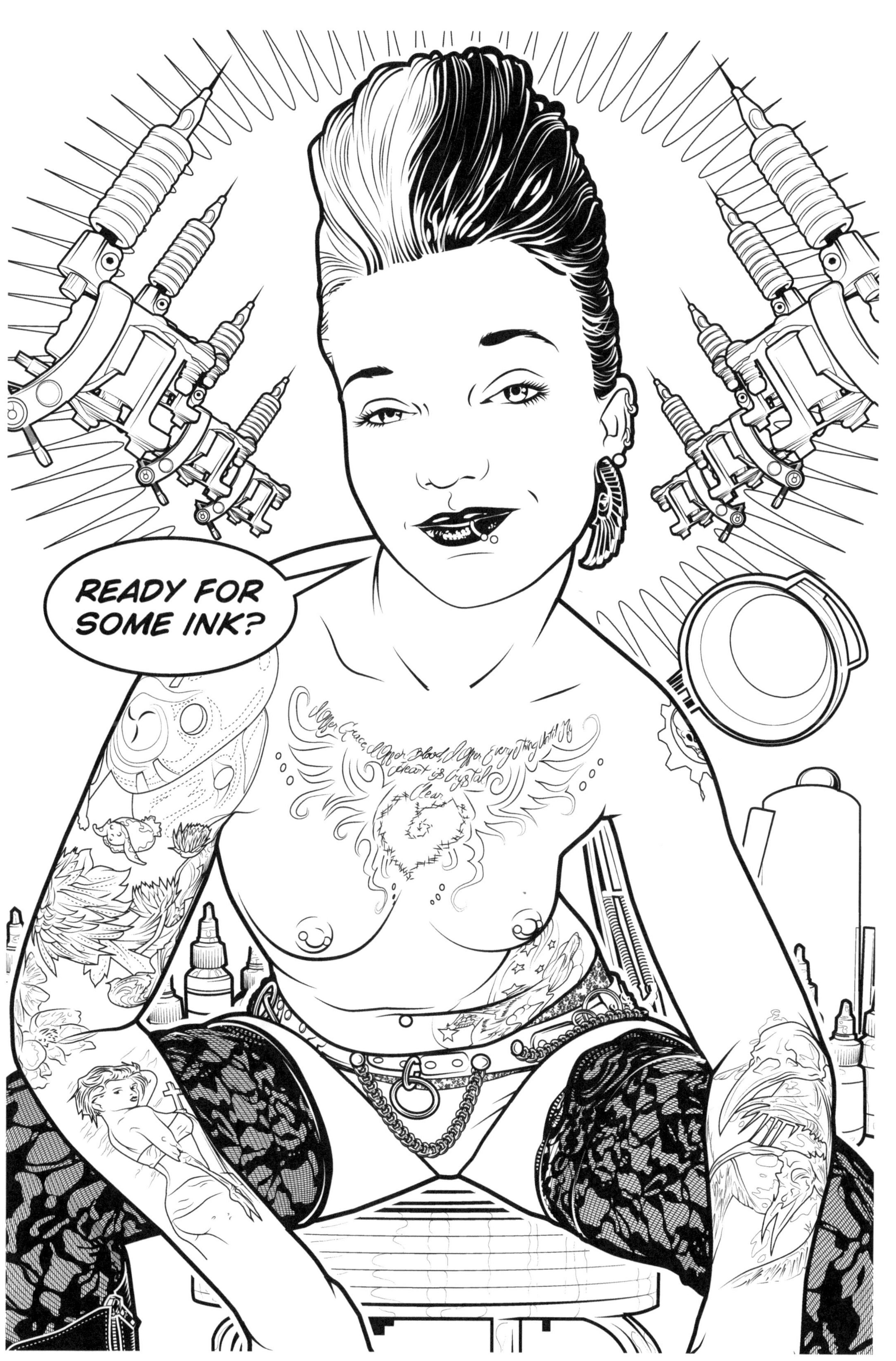
READY FOR SOME INK?

The reference photo of Sade was taken by me on August 1, 2007, at the old Citadel on Mission Street in San Francisco. It was during a photography workshop hosted by Charles Gatewood. For years I felt that I should do something with it. It was one of those images that said different things on different levels. I thought it finally worked best placed in a classic religious context. Though I'm happy with how it came out, I can't help feeling that I'm going to have to answer to the Inquisition at one point for this.

On The Cross

Model: Sade Luna

Reference for the background figures are from the painting, "Christ on the Cross with Saints Vincent Ferrer, John the Baptist, Mark and Antoninus" by Master of the Fiesole Epiphany (Italy, Florence, active circa 1450-1500).

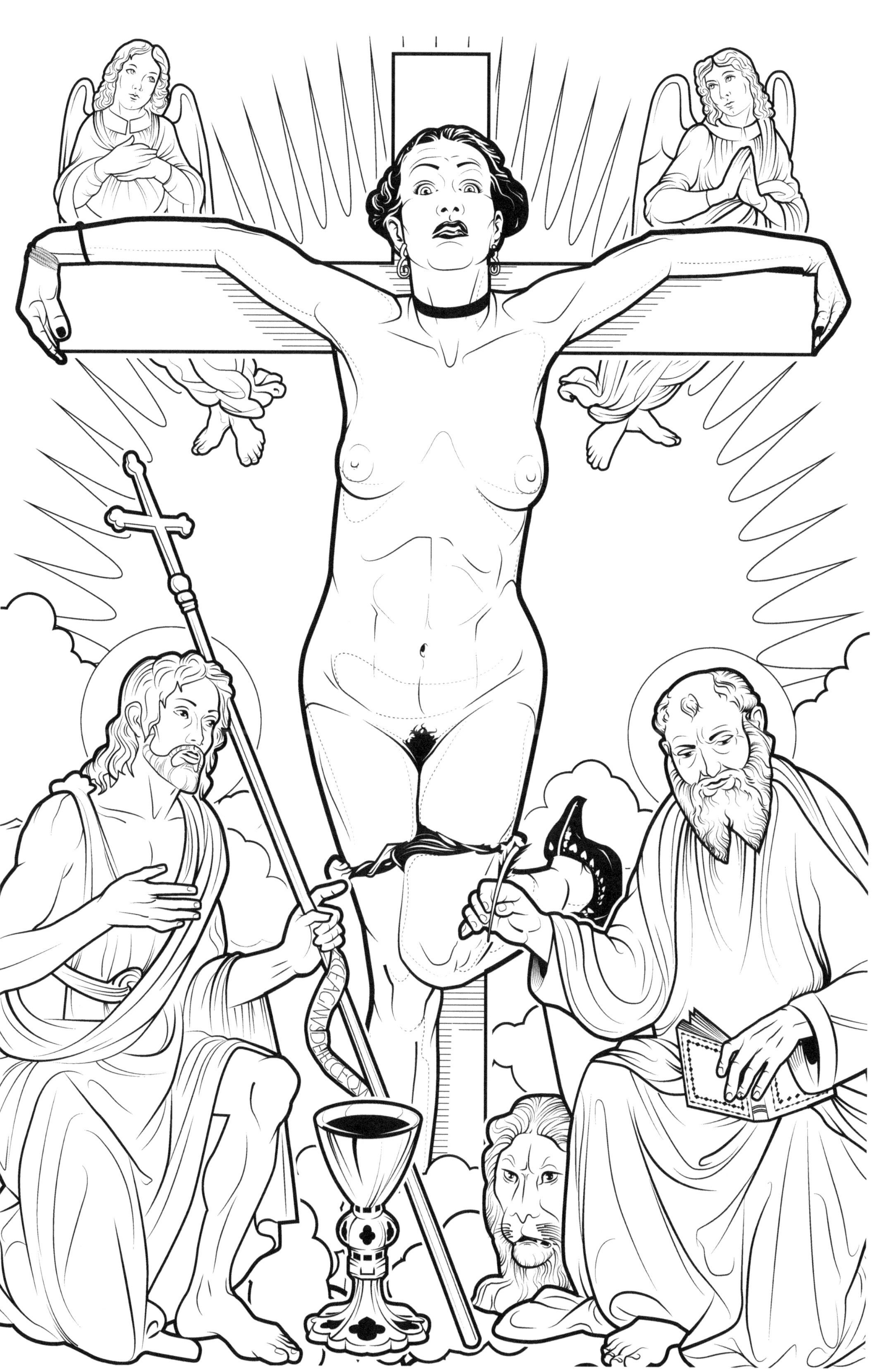

Surely someone around here must have a foot fetish?

Toes

Model: Jenn

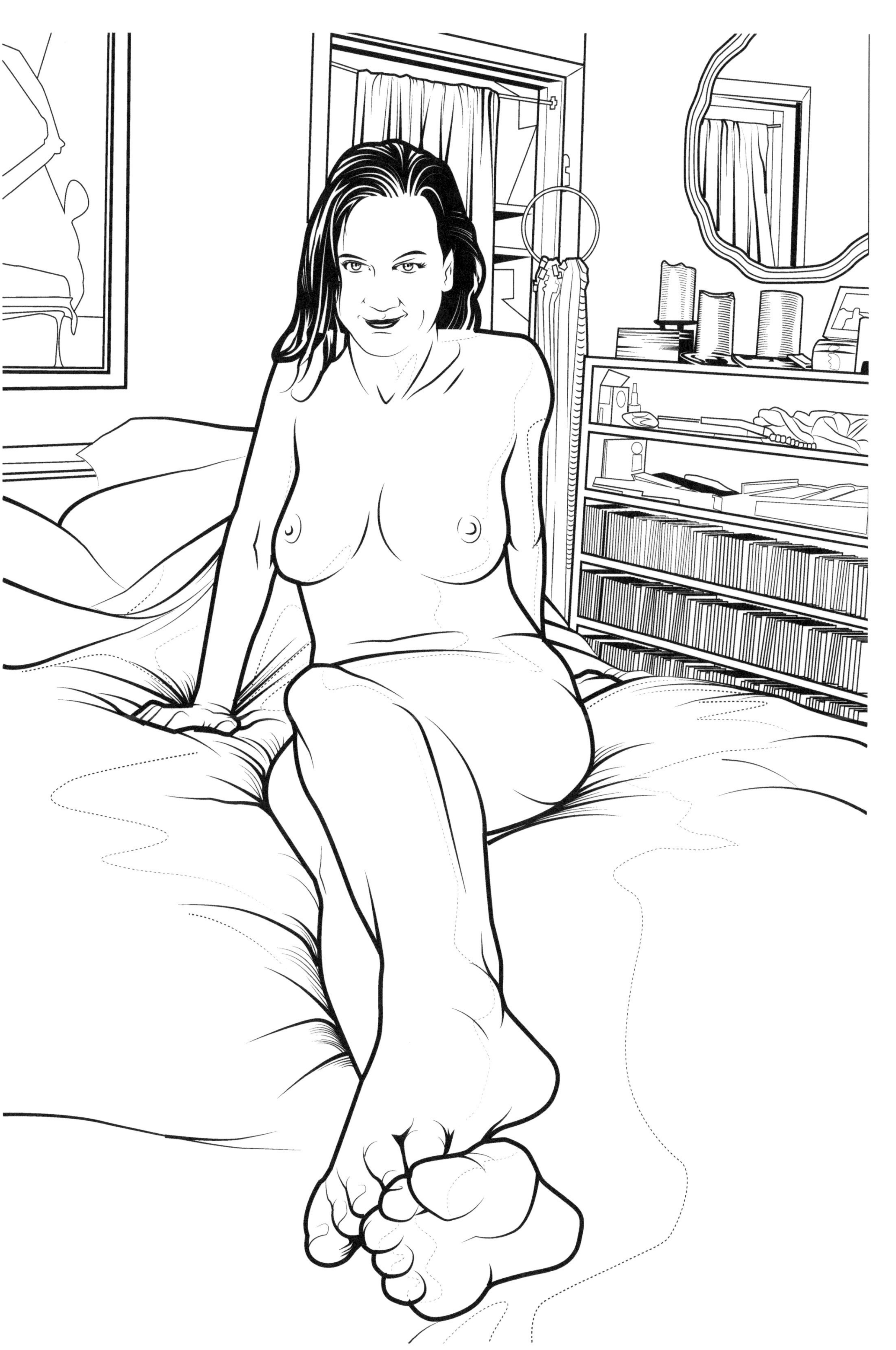

"Face the prisoner towards the window" she ordered, "I want him to stare at what is denied him."

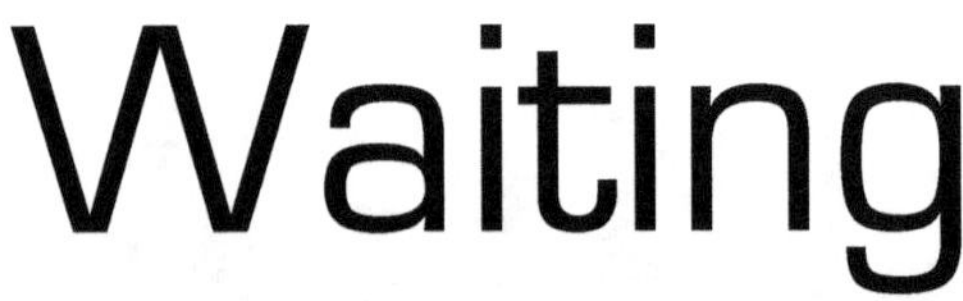

Model: Kory Vixen

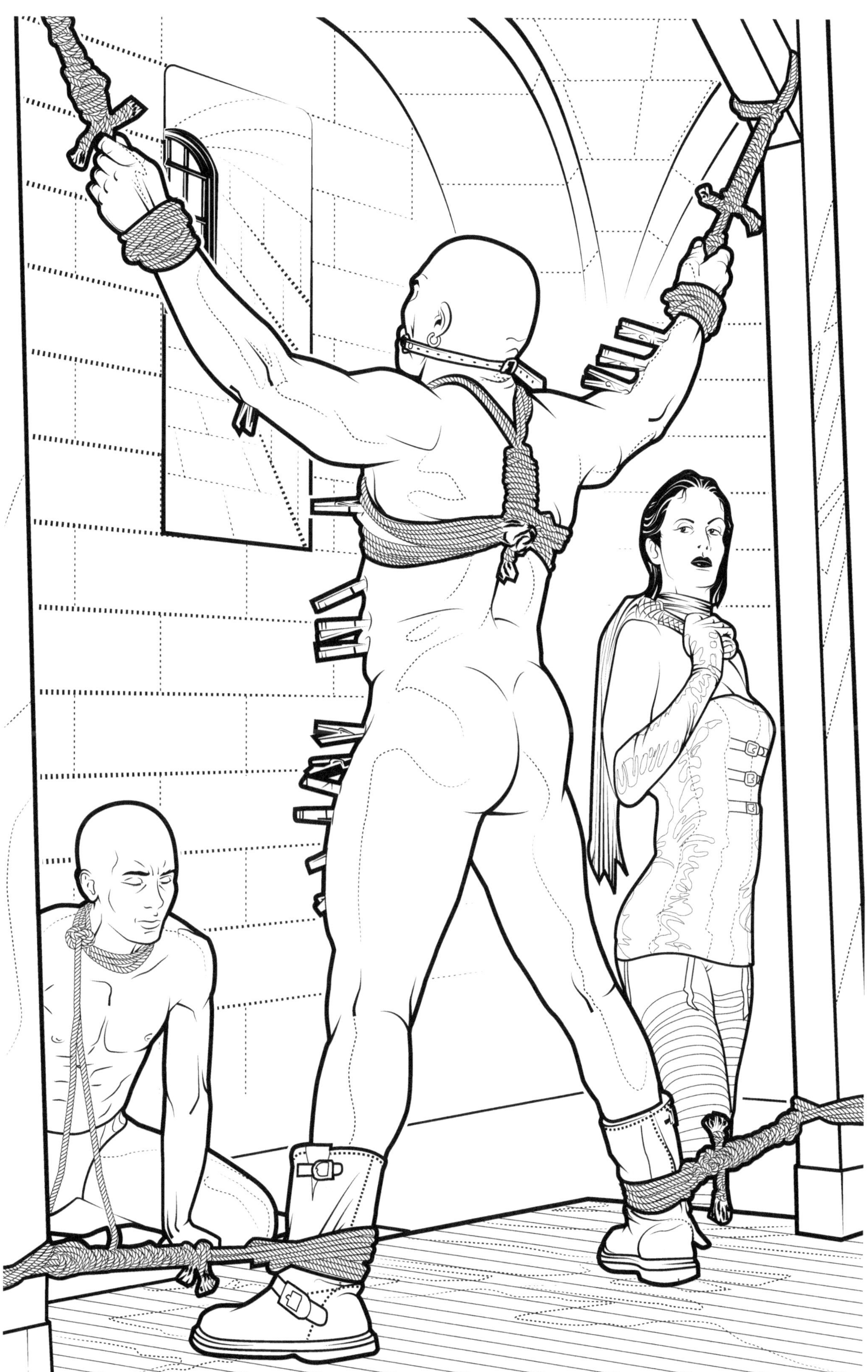

Every once in awhile, someone (usually an attractive if decadent young witch or wizard) decides that it might be nice to play with a dark elder god for a evening.

This, of course, never ends well.

Summoning Cthulhu

Model: FreakyMar5

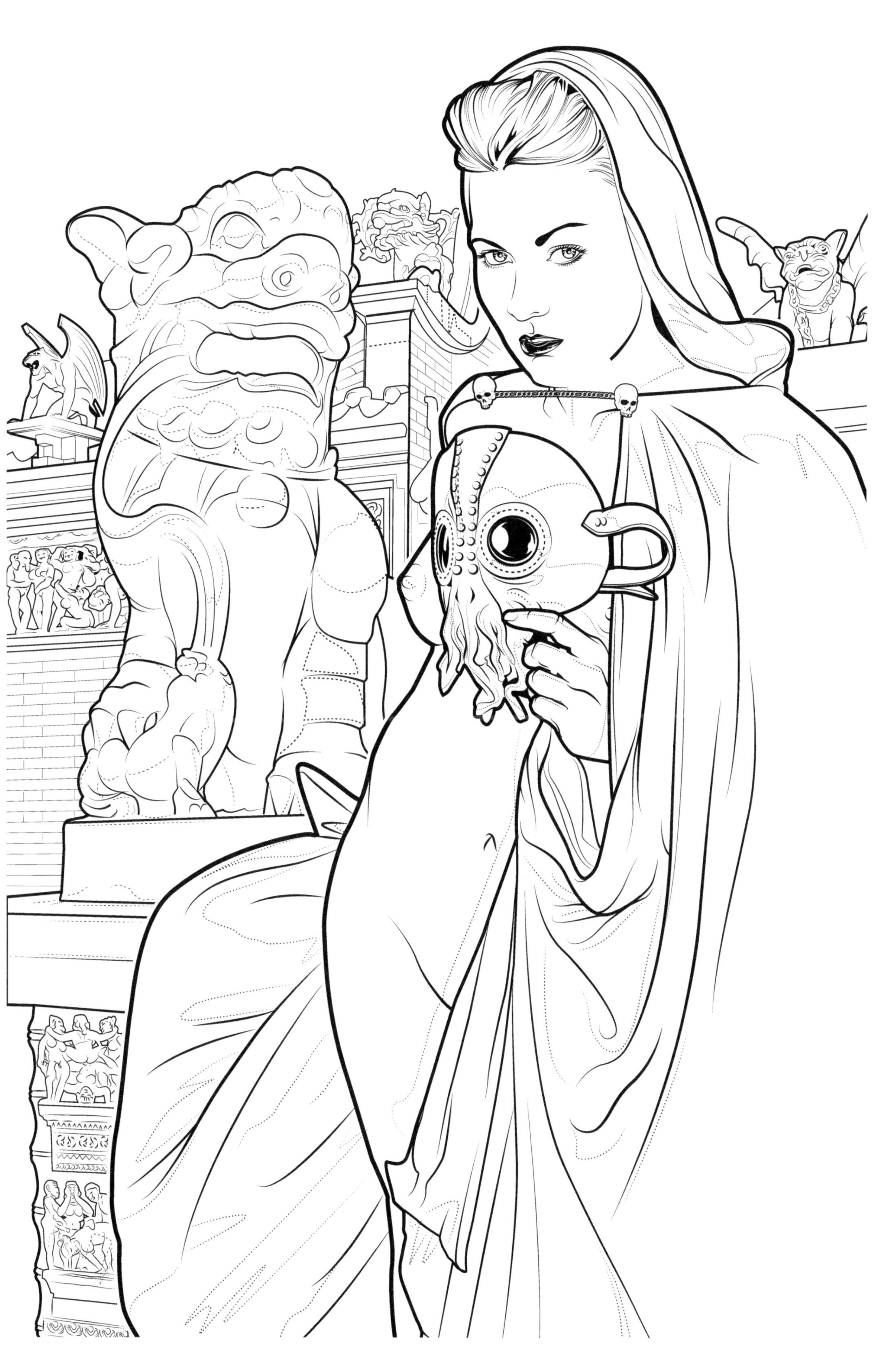

So they then must go forth and find a submissive host in which to insert the spirit of the elder god. Proper effort must be made to prepare the (more often than not) unwilling physical host for Cthulhu.

For many Cthulhu Priestesses, this is considered the really fun part of the job..

Enter Cthulhu

Models: WunderPanties & Freakymar5
Chain Rigging: CorruptMorals

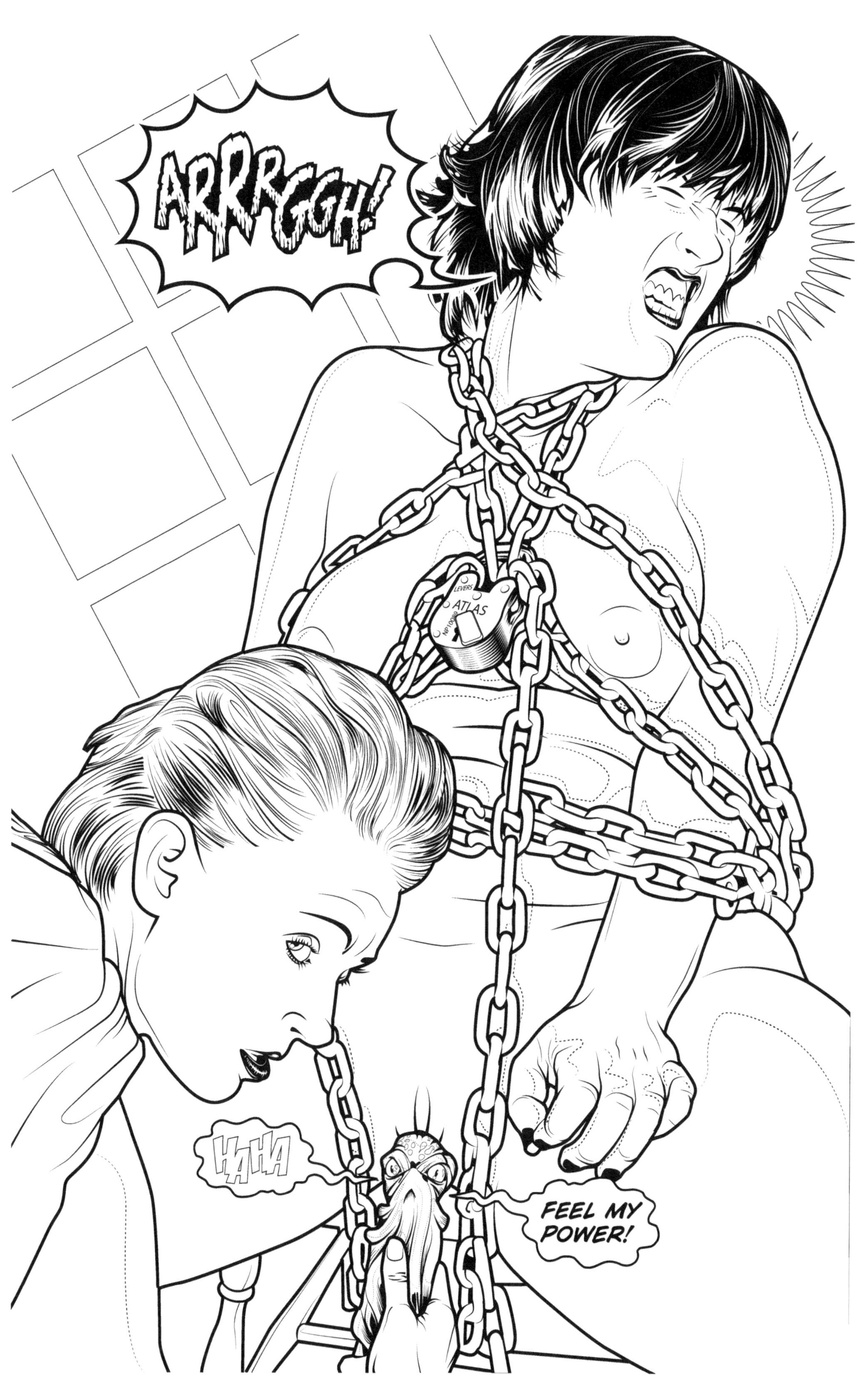
ARRRGGH!
LEVERS
ATLAS
HAHA
FEEL MY POWER!

When the physical host for Cthulhu finally is ready; the Elder God is allowed to possess their body fully!

This is where things usually go wrong!

Cthulhu Rises

Models: WunderPanties & Freakymar5
Chain Rigging: CorruptMorals

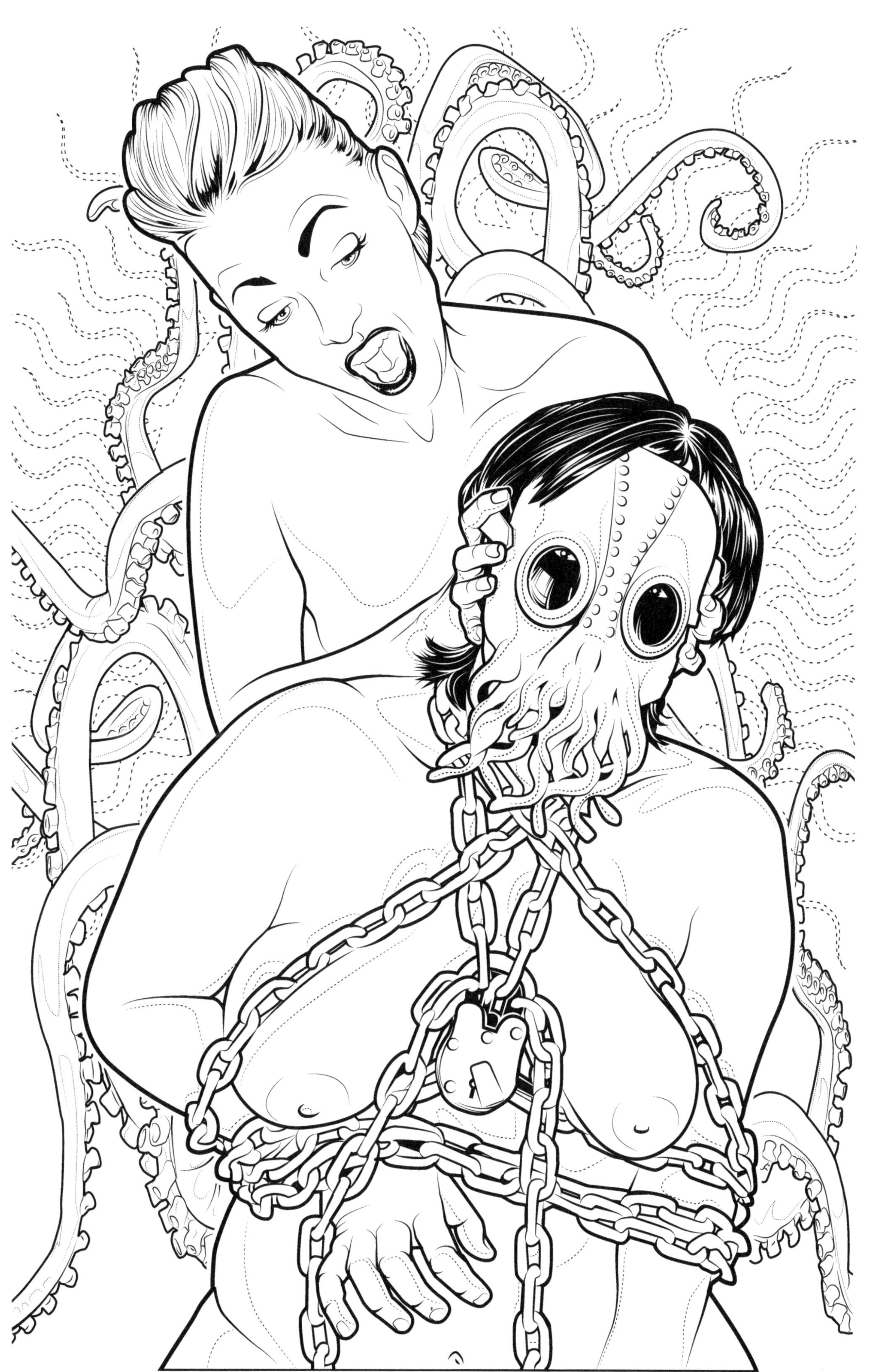

Madness comes in orgasmic waves.
Until death becomes its own form of release.

Cthulhu Attacks

Models: WunderPanties & Freakymar5
Chain Rigging: CorruptMorals

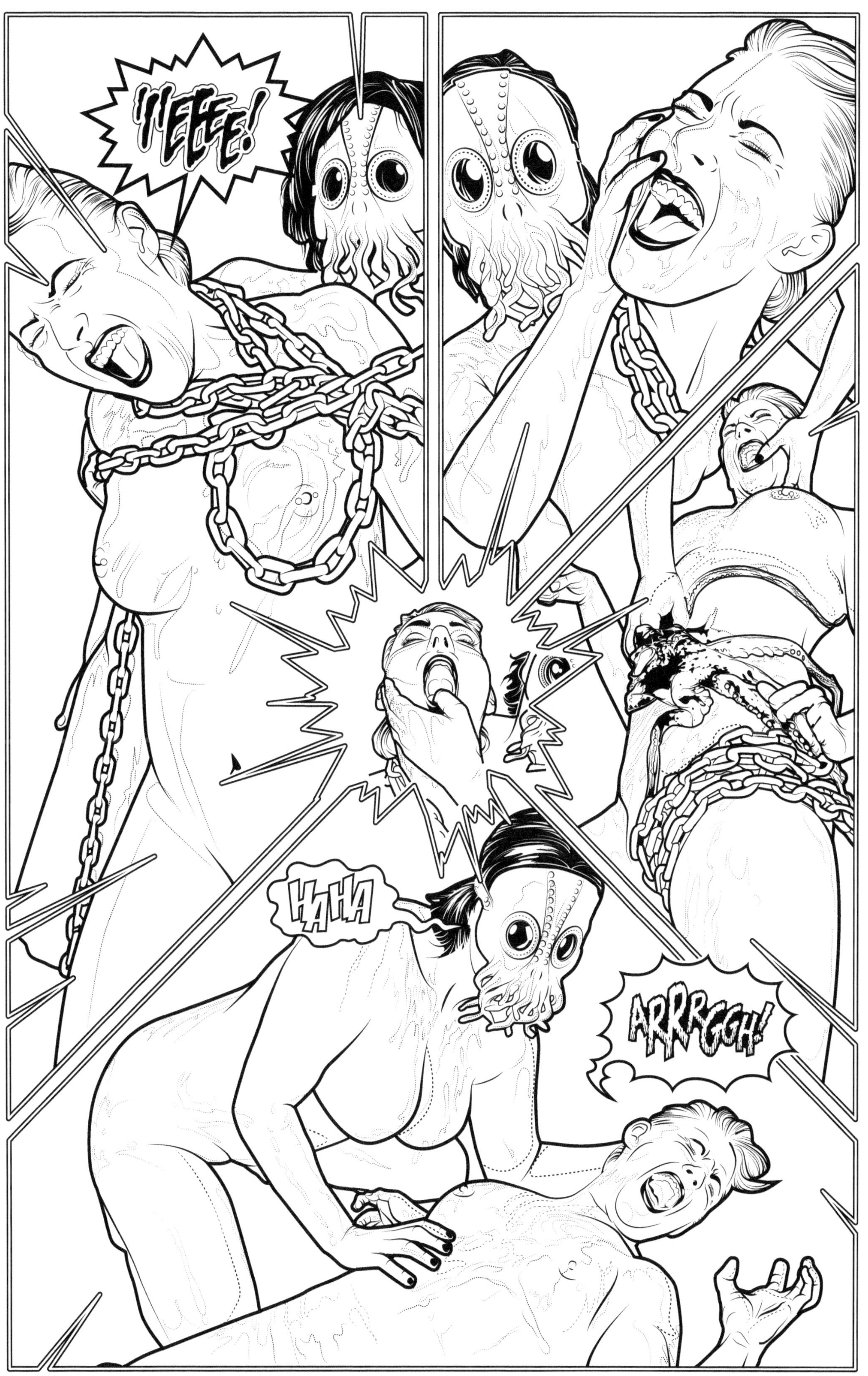

'I'EEEEE!
HAHA
ARRRGGH!

The problem with summoning Cthulhu is that Cthulhu is always happy to visit.

Cthulhu Wins

Models: WunderPanties & Freakymar5

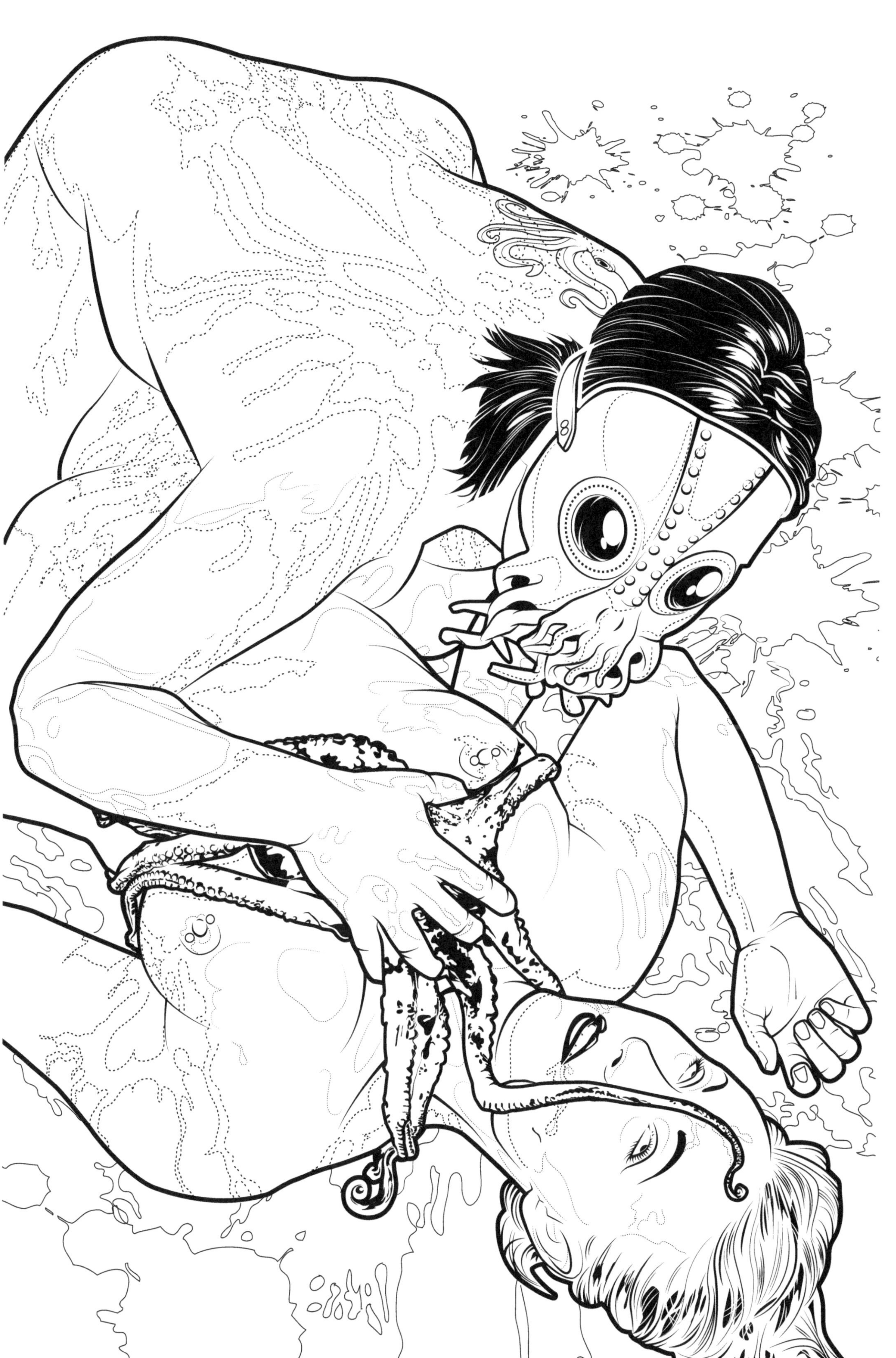

www.ingramcontent.com/pod-product-compliance
Lightning Source LLC
LaVergne TN
LVHW081151110826
845149LV00008B/1617